CALLOWAY CO
7
MURRAY, KY 42071

081997

DISCARD

The
Sara
Summer

CALLOWAY COUNTY PUBLIC LIBRARY
710 Main Street
MURRAY, KY 42071

Other Avon Camelot Books by
Mary Downing Hahn

DAPHNE'S BOOK
THE DEAD MAN IN INDIAN CREEK
THE DOLL IN THE GARDEN
FOLLOWING THE MYSTERY MAN
THE JELLYFISH SEASON
THE SPANISH KIDNAPPING DISASTER
STEPPING ON THE CRACKS
TALLAHASSEE HIGGINS
TIME FOR ANDREW
THE TIME OF THE WITCH
WAIT TILL HELEN COMES

Avon Flare Books

DECEMBER STILLNESS
THE WIND BLOWS BACKWARD

MARY DOWNING HAHN is the author of more than a dozen books for young people, including the award-winning *Stepping on the Cracks*. She is a former children's librarian who lives in Columbia, Maryland, with her husband, Norm.

Avon Books are available at special quantity discounts for bulk purchases for sales promotions, premiums, fund raising or educational use. Special books, or book excerpts, can also be created to fit specific needs.

For details write or telephone the office of the Director of Special Markets, Avon Books, Dept. FP, 1350 Avenue of the Americas, New York, New York 10019, 1-800-238-0658.

The Sara Summer

MARY DOWNING HAHN

AN AVON CAMELOT BOOK

If you purchased this book without a cover, you should be aware that
this book is stolen property. It was reported as "unsold and destroyed"
to the publisher, and neither the author nor the publisher has received
any payment for this "stripped book."

AVON BOOKS
A division of
The Hearst Corporation
1350 Avenue of the Americas
New York, New York 10019

Copyright © 1979 by Mary Downing Hahn
Published by arrangement with Clarion Books, an imprint of Houghton Mifflin
Company
ISBN: 0-380-72354-9
RL: 4.9

All rights reserved, which includes the right to reproduce this book or portions thereof
in any form whatsoever except as provided by the U.S. Copyright Law. For infor-
mation address Houghton Mifflin Company, 215 Park Avenue South, New York,
New York 10003.

First Avon Camelot Printing: July 1995

CAMELOT TRADEMARK REG. U.S. PAT. OFF. AND IN OTHER COUNTRIES, MARCA RE-
GISTRADA, HECHO EN U.S.A.

Printed in the U.S.A.

OPM   10   9   8   7   6   5   4   3   2   1

*For my daughters, Kate and Beth,
whose patience and sense of humor
helped me to complete this book*

ONE

The day I met Sara I was sitting on my front steps sweating in the summer heat and feeling sorry for myself. Not just because I was hot and bored and had nothing to do. No, it was more than that. To begin with, I was twelve years old, and so far it had been a pretty rotten year. Not that eleven was so great, or ten either for that matter. When I think about it, three was probably my best year—that's when I learned to ride a tricycle, started talking in sentences, stopped wetting my bed, and figured out how to use a fork. You don't often learn that many important things in one year.

But before I turned twelve, I used to have a good day now and then, maybe even a week or a month of them in a row. No more. For one thing, on the morning of my twelfth birthday my pituitary gland began to go haywire. I grew five inches in five months, making me five feet, eight inches tall, without gaining a single pound. A stretched-out rubber band is what I resembled most. One straight line from my teeny tiny head to my long skinny toes.

My mother worried all the time about the likely effects my height would have on my social life. She was five foot six herself, and if she was so worried about having a tall daughter, she shouldn't have married a six-foot, three-inch-tall man.

And my friends? Well, even before my pituitary gland started working overtime I was tall for my age, but nobody thought I was weird or anything. I was sort of average. You know, I had a few friends and I got invited to all the important birthday parties and nobody was mean to me or anything. But all that started to change at the sixth-grade Valentine party.

There I was, eating cupcakes, drinking the horrible punch somebody's mother had made, thinking I was having a pretty good day for once. I hadn't been twelve long enough, you see, to know I'd used up all my good days.

Then I opened Froggy's valentine. On the front was a picture of an ugly giraffe, and inside it said:

> *Roses are red,*
> *Violets are blue*
> *A giraffe like you*
> *Belongs in the zoo.*

Now, what's so upsetting about a verse as dumb and unoriginal as that? Plenty if it comes from Froggy. He's the shortest, ugliest, meanest boy in school; the one all the girls hate and all the boys follow around.

Getting a card from him was a sign that I'd been added to his hate list. Like Mary Ann Davison, who weighs over a hundred pounds and wears the same outfit for a week in a row and never washes her hair, I was now a weird and unacceptable person.

Stuffing the valentine into my math book, I tried to eat the rest of my cupcake, but it tasted like styrofoam sprinkled with beebees. On the other side of the room, I could hear Froggy and some of the boys laughing and talking about giraffes getting sick from eating cupcakes, but I didn't look up from my desk. I just sat there staring at the initials somebody had carved on it long before I ever had the misfortune of being in the sixth grade.

As soon as the bell rang I rushed out to my locker, slouched over to look as short as possible, and grabbed my jacket. Hoping to avoid Froggy, I caught up with Maggy Rhodes. Unfortunately, she was walking with Sandy Smith and Ginny Barnett. They were laughing so hard at something Sandy was saying that they barely bothered to say hi to me, but I followed them out the door and across the playground anyway, pretending not to notice that I might as well have been invisible. After all, it was better to be ignored by them than noticed by Froggy.

Actually, I was getting used to being ignored. Maggy had lived next door to me since we were in kindergarden, and until this year I'd always thought of her as my best friend. Lately, though, she'd changed. As long as it was just the two of us, we got along really well, but just let Sandy and Ginny appear on the scene. You wouldn't even know Maggy was the same person. Right away she'd copy Sandy and start acting real sophisticated. If I mentioned something we'd done together, like exploring the creek or making clothes for our Barbie dolls, she'd pretend she didn't know what I was talking about.

But anything was better than walking home alone, so I trotted along beside them listening to them talk about the Valentine party.

Sandy brushed her long blond hair out of her face and smiled eagerly at Maggy. "How many valentines did you get?" she asked in this funny breathless voice she and Ginny have been developing. Although her eyes are naturally huge, she opened them so wide she looked like she had a thyroid condition as she waited for Maggy's reply.

"Seven," Maggy said.

"Only counting boys," Ginny butted in.

"That's what I mean."

"Oh," Ginny said. "I got five." Unlike Sandy,

4

Ginny had little pig eyes, and no matter how hard she tried to make them look wide, the best she could do was squint.

"I got twelve," Sandy said, widening her eyes even more. "One from every single boy in the room. Can you imagine?"

While I was trying to figure out how Ginny, who is both fat and boring, managed to get five valentines, Sandy turned to me. "How many did you get, Emily?" she asked sweetly, as if she already knew the answer.

I smiled and shrugged, but she spotted Froggy's card sticking out of my math book. Before I could stop her, she grabbed it and held it up for everybody to see.

"What's it say? What's it say?" Ginny shrieked, trying to snatch it away from Sandy.

As I lunged toward Sandy, she jumped back and shouted, "Don't let her get it, Mag!"

For a second, Maggy and I looked at each other. I thought she was going to ignore Sandy, but, when Ginny bounced in front of her, waving her arms in my face and laughing, Maggy went into action, too. I guess she didn't want Sandy to think that Ginny was her only loyal friend. With the two of them blocking me, Sandy read the message out loud while Ginny and Maggy howled with laughter.

Too late, I snatched the card and ran down the street, leaving them behind me. The last thing I heard was Maggy shouting, "What's the matter, Emily, can't you take a joke?"

After that, things weren't really the same between Maggy and me. Even when Sandy and Ginny weren't there, she never wanted to do anything except sit around and talk about boys, a subject that bored me to death. To make it worse, she started talking in a soft little breathy voice like Sandy's and widening her eyes. Maggy really began to get on my nerves, but every time I accused her of trying to be like Sandy, she got mad and said I was immature. If I'd had any sense, I would have started looking for another friend. But I kept hoping Maggy would get tired of following Sandy and Ginny around and start acting like her old self again.

So all spring I hung around, trying to laugh when Sandy said things like, "Don't get your neck caught in the telephone lines, Emily," or "Just think, if the streetlights burn out, they can ask Emily to change them. She won't even need a ladder." It was pretty depressing trying to convince everybody that I had a great sense of humor when I didn't. Every joke hurt my feelings, and the more I laughed, the more jokes Sandy came up with.

By the time summer vacation started, I had just about given up. The only solution was to stay away from Sandy, so I started sleeping as late as possible and spending most of my afternoons lying in the hammock in our backyard. Sometimes I read, but a lot of the time I just lay there with the book in my lap and stared up into the trees, worrying about everything from the length of my legs to the possibility of dying from leukemia.

Just when I thought I had detected at least five of cancer's warning signs, I learned that someone had bought old Mrs. Murphy's house. It had been vacant since April, when her son put Mrs. Murphy in a nursing home, and my mother and father had worried a lot about the sort of people who might buy it. Unlike the other houses in College Hills, Mrs. Murphy's house was an old rambling Victorian mansion with a big front porch and a cupola on the side. About twenty years ago, Mrs. Murphy sold the land around it and surrounded herself with dozens of tidy little brick colonials like the one my family lived in.

To me, Mrs. Murphy's house looked like a stately ocean liner surrounded by tugboats, but my father thought it was a disgrace to the neighborhood. He said he'd hate to pay the heating bills, and my mother said the plumbing was primitive. They were both afraid that a group of students from the university would buy it and turn it into a commune and play loud rock music all night and sell marijuana to the kids in the neighborhood.

Anyway, the day I saw a U-Haul van pull up in the

7

front yard, I decided to give the old hammock a break and watch our new neighbors unload their stuff. I sat on the steps listening to people shouting and thumping, hoping I might get a glimpse of something interesting.

I didn't have long to wait. First I heard a terrible scream and then this little kid came flying around the side of the house. She was so scrawny I could almost count the ribs sticking out below her halter, but she was running like the Roadrunner himself and shrieking at the same time.

Close behind her came an older girl about my age, waving a baseball bat. "I'll get you, Hairball!" the older girl yelled as the little kid ducked under a low-hanging limb and disappeared behind the house.

Still hollering, the older girl followed her, leaving me sitting on my steps watching the limb sway back and forth and listening to the shouts from the backyard. Loud and clear, I heard the girl scream a word I'm not supposed to know, let alone say out loud. Then a man's voice shouted, "Sara, leave Jennifer alone and get in here and help your mother!"

Someone squealed, a screen door slammed three times and for several minutes it sounded like a whole bunch of people were shouting and screaming all at once. Above the racket, I could hear a dog barking frantically.

Across the street, Mrs. Boardman came outside with

8

a watering can and started sprinkling the roses that grew between her yard and the Murphy's yard. It was the third time she'd watered them since the U-Haul arrived, so I had a feeling she was just as curious about the new people as I was.

As soon as she went back inside, I got up and walked over to the hedge on the edge of our front lawn. I was hoping the girl with the bat would come back outside, but I wasn't sure I'd have the nerve to introduce myself.

TWO

The sound of a door banging startled me. There was Sara on the front steps, but this time it was me she was frowning at, not Hairball.

"If you're so interested in my house," she called, "why don't you come over here and get a better look?"

She didn't look very friendly, standing there squinting in the sunlight, and I felt tempted to pretend I hadn't heard her. But my curiosity overcame my fear and, instead of turning around and running into my house, I came out from behind our hedge and crossed the street. As soon as I put my foot on her property, the dog I'd heard earlier came charging around the side of the house, barking and growling. Without even thinking, I grabbed a limb and swung myself up into the maple tree in the corner of Sara's yard. From a safe seat about six feet off the ground, I watched Sara trying to get a grip on the dog's collar.

"Frank!" she shouted. "Cut it out!"

But Frank paid no attention to her. Watching him leap at the tree trunk, I tried to remember if dogs could climb trees. Just as I was getting ready to move to a higher limb, Sara managed to pull him down on the ground.

"Sit! Sit!" she shouted, holding his collar with one hand and slapping his hindquarters with the other.

Gurgling and gasping, his eyes popping from his head as he strained against the collar, Frank ignored Sara. He seemed to have only one thing on his mind: to tear me limb from limb.

Looking up at me, Sara said, "He won't hurt you. You can come down now."

Trying to ignore the scorn in her voice, I looked at Frank. He was still snarling and baring his teeth in an ugly way. "Actually, it's pretty comfortable up here," I said. "Cooler. More of a breeze."

She shrugged. "You can sit there all day if you want to. But since it's my tree you're sitting in, maybe you'd like to tell me your name."

"Emily Sherwood. What's yours?"

"Sara Slater."

"Oh."

We stared at each other for what seemed a very long

11

CALLOWAY COUNTY PUBLIC LIBRARY
710 Main Street
MURRAY, KY 42071

time. Frantically I tried to think of something to say, but as usual my mind was a blank.

"Where's your sister?" I finally asked.

"How do you know I have a sister?"

Her tone of voice made me wonder if she'd given Hairball or Jennifer or whatever the kid's name was a fatal blow in the backyard. For all I knew, her parents were at this very minute burying the body in the basement and hoping they could keep it a secret from the neighbors.

"I saw you chasing her around the house a little while ago," I admitted, hoping my confession wouldn't prompt her to go inside and get the bat to finish me off.

"Oh, her. That was Hairball." She spat the name out in a way that made it clear we were discussing a subhuman species, not someone who could possibly be mistaken for a sister.

"That's a funny name," I said.

"That's what she is," Sara said. "She picks her nose, sucks her thumb, wets the bed, and has the mange."

Grabbing a limb, Sara climbed up into the tree next to me. Up close, she was kind of ugly. And not too clean. Her face was pale and splotched with freckles, and her long dark hair was braided so tightly it made her ears stick out. Her skin was so white that the veins in her arms and legs could have been painted on with a tiny paintbrush dipped in blue. And she was tall and thin. Every part of her was long-arms, legs, toes, hands, feet.

"How tall are you?" I blurted out. I had to know.

"Five foot nine," she said. "And still growing."

I smiled. "I'm five foot eight." She had me beat by a whole inch!

"I guess that makes you feel just great." She scowled at me.

"What's an inch?" I asked, trying to pretend that height meant nothing to me. Then, to change the subject, I asked her where she used to live.

"New York City." She frowned at the quiet green lawns surrounding us and the well-kept houses nesting comfortably in beds of flowers and shrubbery. "And I'm sorry we left. This place looks like an overcrowded Monopoly board."

"Oh, College Hills is okay," I said. "The shopping center is just a few blocks away and there's a swimming pool across the train tracks and the university is real close. And we're only a few miles from Washington, D.C.," I added, thinking she might be impressed by a city as important as Washington.

"I've been there a million times," Sara said. "Next to New York, Washington is a real nothing place." She sighed. "Is it always this hot here?"

"Only in the summer," I said, trying to make her laugh.

Sara didn't even smile. "Want to go inside and have a glass of Kool-Aid?"

I nodded. I was hot and thirsty and I'd always wanted to see what the Murphy's house was like inside. Until now, the closest I'd gotten was the front door when Maggy and I had gone there to trick-or-treat. Mrs. Murphy had never asked us in. She didn't like kids very much.

As soon as my feet touched the ground, Frank got up from the hole he'd dug by the front porch and started walking toward me, growling softly. Coward that I am, I froze, but Sara stamped her foot at him, and he settled back down in the dust.

"Frank's a funny name for a dog," I said after we'd closed the screen door, leaving him safely outside.

"It's short for Frankenstein," Sara said. "He's put together from a lot of different breeds."

"Oh, yeah." I laughed, stopping myself just in time from saying that explained why he was so ugly.

Still laughing, I walked right into a woman coming down the hall and knocked the boxes she was carrying all over the place. I was so embarrassed I kept apologizing like a broken record the whole time I was picking up the boxes. At first I didn't even realize that the person I was helping was Sara's mother. I thought she was her sister. Not Hairball, but an older one. For one thing, Mrs. Slater was shorter than I was, and she was wearing ragged cut-off jeans and a baggy T-shirt.

Plus she was barefoot, her hair was pulled back in two frizzy yellow pigtails, and she wasn't wearing lipstick. In College Hills, mothers just didn't look like that.

It wasn't until Sara introduced us that I realized her mother wasn't just another kid. While I stood there turning as red as a July sunset, Mrs. Slater seized my hand and shook it.

"I'm so glad to meet you, Emily," she said. "I can just tell that you and Sara are going to be great friends. You look enough alike to be sisters. Twins almost. Same height, same coloring. Even the same freckles!"

Not knowing what to say, I just blushed and giggled nervously. But I wanted to cry. Hadn't I just thought a few minutes ago that Sara was ugly? And here I was being told we looked exactly alike.

"Can we have some Kool-Aid?" Sara asked.

Still holding my hand, Mrs. Slater said, "Kool-Aid? Well, I'm not sure if I have any, but I'll look."

While her mother rattled things in the kitchen, Sara led me around the house and told me about New York and the great private school she'd gone to and her visits to museums, the zoo, the Statue of Liberty, the Empire State Building, the United Nations Building, and all sorts of other places I'd never even heard of. By the time Mrs. Slater reappeared with the Kool-Aid, I was more convinced than ever that I had led one of the most boring lives in the whole country.

As Mrs. Slater set our glasses in front of us, Hairball

stepped out from behind her and moved hesitantly toward the table.

"Get out of here, Hairball!" Sara said fiercely.

"You're not drinking yours here. Take it out on the back porch or something."

"Oh, Sara," Mrs. Slater said in a sort of sad voice.

Looking at Sara nervously, Hairball slid into a chair across the table and regarded me with eyes that made Sandy look half blind. Her face was pale and small, kind of like an old-fashioned china doll, and her hair was yellow and curly and so tangled I wondered if it had ever been combed. She reminded me of a fairy princess, fragile and elflike. She didn't look at all like Sara. Or me.

Not ready to give up, Sara glared at her mother. "She slurps when she drinks and her nose is always running. How can I enjoy my Kool-Aid if I have to look at her while I'm drinking it?"

"Sara, please," Mrs. Slater said. Looking at me, she said, "I'm sure Emily doesn't mind having her Kool-Aid with Jennifer, do you?"

Trying not to offend anyone, I shrugged and smiled. I couldn't understand why Mrs. Slater was asking me; if I ever acted like that, I knew what my mother would do. Send my guest home and me to my room. Being rude to my little brother was simply not tolerated.

"Delores!" a man shouted from upstairs. "Come up here and help me with these bed frames. Do you

16

expect me to do everything around here?''

Mrs. Slater started for the stairs. "Behave yourself, Sara," she said before she rushed out of the dining room, tripped over something, and ran on upstairs.

Ignoring the dirty look Sara was giving me for siding with her mother, I picked up my glass and took a big swallow of Kool-Aid. "Ugh!" I choked and spit it back into the glass.

Staring at me strangely, Sara took a tiny sip of hers and made a face. "She must have forgotten to put the sugar in."

Sara got up and went into the kitchen. I could hear her rummaging in boxes and opening cabinet doors. I looked at Hairball and she looked at me, her face a blank. She didn't seem to be much of a talker.

"How old are you?" I asked, trying to be polite.

"Six." She put her thumb in her mouth and sucked it slowly and deliberately, never taking her eyes off my face.

"My brother, Jamie, will be six soon. Maybe you could be friends."

She shrugged and smiled around her thumb. I was starting to feel like an idiot.

Just then Sara slammed a sugar bowl down on the table. "If you think her Kool-Aid is bad, try staying for supper sometime. I'd eat out every night if I could."

After dumping three heaping spoonfuls of sugar into

her glass, Sara handed me the bowl and the dripping spoon. When I was finished, I started to pass the bowl to Hairball, who had been sitting there quietly sucking her thumb and staring at me, but Sara grabbed it.

"Don't give any to her. She likes it without sugar, don't you, Hairball?"

Hairball didn't say anything. She just stared at her glass. She was so pitiful-looking, I couldn't help feeling sorry for her. As if she sensed my feelings, Hairball turned her eyes to me, took her thumb out of her mouth, and reached for the sugar bowl.

"Oh no you don't." Sara cracked her across the knuckles with the spoon. "Sugar is bad for your teeth, don't you know that? Drink your nice Kool-Aid just the way Mommy fixed it for you. She knows what's best for little Hairball."

Obediently Hairball sipped her Kool-Aid and spit it out. "It tastes bad, Sara," she whined. "I want some sugar in it."

"Think you can get it?" Sara stood up and held the bowl over her head.

Hairball ran around the table and started jumping for the bowl like a trained monkey, but she couldn't get near it.

"Say please, Hairball, say pretty pretty pretty please with honey and sugar on it," Sara commanded. She was laughing so hard at Hairball's antics that she could hardly say it.

Although I had been a little shocked when Sara started teasing Hairball, I couldn't help thinking she looked pretty funny hopping around and trying to repeat Sara's words. And Sara had such a crazy snorty laugh that it was hard for me not to start laughing too. Then Hairball knocked over her glass and the Kool-Aid ran across the table and into my lap. I jumped up and my chair fell over, sending a cat I hadn't noticed before running for cover. That got me laughing so hard I got Kool-Aid up my nose and started snorting like a horse having a fit.

While Hairball stood there laughing and crying at the same time, Sara grabbed an old toy rabbit and we ran all around the house with it tossing it back and forth over Hairball's head.

Finally somebody upstairs shouted, "You kids shut up!" and I decided it was time for me to go home before I got into trouble with Sara's parents.

THREE

As I raced up our front steps, I saw Mother frowning at me through the screen door.

"Where have you been, Emily? Didn't you hear me calling you?" she asked.

I shook my head. "I was across the street at the Slaters' house.

She brightened right up when she heard that. "Oh? What are they like?"

"Well, there's a girl my age. Her name is Sara and she's even taller than I am. Can you believe that? And a little kid, her sister I guess, and her name is Jennifer, only Sara calls her Hairball. She's Jamie's age. And they have a dog named Frankenstein, Frank for short. He barks a lot."

As I stopped to catch my breath, Mother asked me what Mr. and Mrs. Slater were like.

"Well, she's real short, she looks like a kid, and

she's a terrible cook. She forgot to put sugar in the Kool-Aid. I didn't see him, he was upstairs putting bed frames together or something.''

"What does he do?'' Mother asked.

"Do? His job? I don't know, Sara didn't say.'' Sometimes I think my mother is interested in the most boring things about people. Who cares whether someone's father works for the government in some office (like my father) or pumps gas in a filling station? My mother does, that's who. Would you believe that I made friends with a girl when I was in second grade and after my mother found out that her father was a trash collector she refused to let me play with her?

"Do you think they'll take care of poor old Mrs. Murphy's flowers?'' Mother went on. "She was so proud of them.''

"Oh, sure.'' I didn't have the heart to tell her that Frank had already dug up most of the peonies. When I'd left, they were scattered all over the lawn, and he was hard at work on the azaleas behind them.

Mother handed me the silverware. "Please set the table, Emily,'' she said. "Well, I hope the Slaters will be all right. At least a bunch of college students didn't move in.''

After I set the table, Mother sent me outside to get Jamie out of the sandbox. As usual, he put up a terrific struggle, but I finally dragged him into the bathroom and stuck his hands under the cold water. As I scrubbed the sand off, I calmed him down a little by telling him about Hairball.

"One thing about her," I added as he squirmed away from the washcloth, "she always does what her sister tells her to. Always. And you know why? If she doesn't, her sister beats her up. What do you think of that?"

"I think I don't like her sister very much," Jamie said, wiggling away from me before I could dry his hands.

I shook my head. It would be awfully hard to get Jamie into shape. Thanks to Mother's strict rules about fighting, I'd been nice to him for too long.

At dinner, Mother tried to tell Daddy about the Slaters, but he was more interested in a revolution in some country that only he and the newscaster had ever heard of. I felt like telling him that Mr. Slater made his living selling drugs. That would have gotten his attention.

While I was loading the dishwasher, Maggy's mother came over and suggested that she and mother take a cake to the Slaters'. To welcome them to the neighborhood, she said, but she didn't fool me. What she really wanted was an excuse to see for herself what the Slaters were like.

I followed them out to the front porch and

22

watched them cross the street. They were both wearing polyester shorts and striped T-shirts, the mix-and-match type that Sears sells. Their hair was short and tightly curled, their makeup was freshly applied, and their clothes were premapressed and wrinkle-free. As I watched them step into the shadow of the maple tree in Sara's yard, I wondered what they would think of Mrs. Slater's outfit and her frizzy pigtails.

While I was sitting on the steps, I saw Maggy come outside and duck under the dogwood tree between our house and hers.

"Hi, Emily," shc said hesitantly.

"What do you want?" I asked in a nasty tone of voice. I didn't want her to think I'd been sitting around all summer pining for her company.

"I just felt like coming over. You don't have to get mad about it, do you?" Her voice didn't sound too pleasant either, but she sat down next to me.

"You haven't been over here once all summer," I said.

"Well, I'm here now, aren't I?"

Since I certainly couldn't argue about that, I waited for her to reveal her reason for honoring me with her presence. Maybe she'd finally gotten sick of Sandy and Ginny and talking about boys all the time.

"I was wondering about the people who bought the Murphy's house," she finally said. "Have you met them yet? Mom says they have a daughter our age and I wondered if you'd seen her or anything. Sandy and Ginny and I were at the pool all day, so I haven't been home.''

We both looked over at the Slaters' house, and I felt kind of important. ''Sure I saw her. I spent the whole afternoon over there, as a matter of fact. Her name is Sara, and she's really nice.'' Then I paused. What else could I tell Maggy? I was pretty sure she wouldn't like Sara.

''Well, what's she like?'' Maggy asked.

''She's tall and thin, even taller than I am, she wears her hair in braids, and she used to live in New York City.''

''Is she pretty?''

''Not very.''

''Oh. Well, what does she like to do? Does she know how to dance? Does she have a boyfriend?''

I shook my head. ''She doesn't look like the type to dance or have boyfriends,'' I said.

Maggy sat there silently for a few seconds, thinking about what I'd told her. ''Well,'' she said at last. ''Introduce me to her tomorrow, okay?''

''Sure.''

After Maggy left, I went inside and turned on the television set. Daddy was upstairs trying to put Jamie to bed, so I had the living room to myself.

When I was sure that Jamie was asleep, I went

upstairs and got in bed. Since I wasn't very sleepy, I started to read "The Tell-Tale Heart," by Edgar Allan Poe, but after a couple of pages I started hearing my own heart thumping away. I got so scared I put the book on the floor and lay there with my light on listening to the Rhodeses' air conditioner roaring on and off and trying not to think about my heart.

When I heard Mother and Daddy coming up the stairs, I turned out my light and pretended to be asleep.

"When Wanda and I went inside, we were a little shocked," I heard Mother say through the open door of their room. "The whole place was in chaos and the kids were running around fighting and screaming at each other. There were two cats on the dining-room table licking the plates, and a dog was growling at us from under the couch."

Daddy laughed.

"Mr. Slater was barely civil to us," Mother said. "He disappeared as soon as we walked in the door. Said he had a lot of reading to do before the university opens. He teaches English."

"English." My father repeated the word like it was a disease too awful to discuss in polite society. "He's probably a Democrat."

"You should see her. Dressed like a teenager and totally disorganized. They look like a pair of aging hippies."

"Oh, God, they'll probably rent rooms to college students," Daddy muttered. "You wait. Any night now we'll be blasted out of our beds with hi-fis. There'll be loud parties, drugs, an no place to park the car."

"I know. That's just what Wanda and I said. But what really bothers me is the way the kids act. When Mrs. Slater told the older girl to leave her sister alone and go to bed, the girl's response was incredible. Wanda and I were embarrassed to death. If Emily or Maggy ever spoke to us like that, they'd spend their teenage years in their rooms."

Oh no, I thought, why did Sara have to put on a show for Mother? Now she'd probably never let me associate with her.

"You don't think she'll be a bad influence on Emily, do you?" Mother asked Daddy. "You know what a follower Emily is. All she needs is someone like Sara to imitate."

Unfortunately one of them closed their door at that point and I couldn't hear Daddy's reply. I rolled over, congratulating myself on having known in advance exactly how they would react to the Slaters, but a little disappointed in Mother's assumption that Sara would be a bad influence on me. After all, if I were a totally spineless person, I would still be following Sandy around, coating my mouth with lip gloss, smearing my cheeks with blusher, and decorating my walls with rock star posters. For all Mother knew, I might turn out to be a bad influence on Sara. Why not?

FOUR

The next morning I was sitting at the kitchen table eating my Cheerios and trying to finish "The Tell-Tale Heart." In the morning sunlight, it didn't seem quite so horrifying, but it was still pretty bad. When the doorbell rang, I jumped about a foot off my chair.

I heard Mother switch off the vacuum cleaner and answer the door. "Emily, Sara's here," she called and started vacuuming again.

Embarrassed at being caught in my pajamas with half my buttons missing and my hair a tangled mess, I started running upstairs, but I wasn't fast enough.

"Aren't you dressed yet?" Sara asked, intercepting me at the foot of the steps. Her hair was neatly braided, but she was wearing the same shirt and shorts she'd had on yesterday.

"Wait here, I'll be ready in a minute." I dashed upstairs to my room, pulled on the clothes I'd left in a heap on the floor last night and ran back down.

Sara was standing by the kitchen table, my book in her hand. "Haven't you read this before?" she asked. "I read it years ago. It's pretty good." She laid the book down, losing my place. "But it's nothing compared to *The Bloodville Horror or The Curse of the Bloodsuckers or Night Scream*. Have you read them?"

I shook my head. How could I tell her that my mother allowed me to read nothing that wasn't available in the children's room at the library? To make sure I wasn't tempted to sneak over to the adult section, she had even marked my library card "children's room material only."

"Want me to loan you one?"

I shook my head again and forced myself to tell her that I wasn't allowed to read books like that.

Sara gave me a funny look. "My parents don't believe in censoring my reading material," she said. "And even if they did, I certainly wouldn't pay any attention to them. I'd read whatever I wanted to."

As we started out the back door, my mother stopped me. "Where are you going, Emily?" she asked.

"Nowhere. Just bike riding," I said.

"You weren't intending to leave the house looking like that, were you?"

Not daring to look at Sara, I ran back upstairs to change my clothes. Why was my mother so tactless? Didn't she realize that she had just insulted Sara? After all, compared to Sara I looked like a model of neatness, and there Mother was criticizing my appearance.

In a frenzy, I yanked off the T-shirt and pulled on one without a Kool-Aid stain down the front. I was terrified that Sara might have left in disgust. Why would someone whose mother let her read what she wanted and wear what she pleased want to be friends with me?

When I came downstairs, Sara was sitting at the kitchen table with Mother, drinking a cup of coffee and telling her what a good book *The Bloodville Horror* was.

"It doesn't have any sex in it," Sara was saying, "and hardly any profanity."

Mother raised her eyebrows at me. I was afraid Sara wasn't making the impression she thought she was.

"Are you ready to go, Em?" Sara asked.

With a quick look at Mother, who was staring thoughtfully at Sara, I nodded.

"My bike's out front," Sara said, getting up.

"I'll meet you," I said.

Pulling my bike out of the shed, I pedaled around the side of the house.

"Is that your bike or your mother's? It doesn't even have gears." Sara was sitting on a gorgeous yellow ten-speed, the kind I'd give anything, including Jamie to own.

"My father won't let me have a ten-speed. Or even

a three-speed. He thinks they're dangerous."

"I wouldn't be caught dead on an old-lady's bike like that one," Sara said.

She pedaled out into the street, her gears clicking, and I followed her, wondering if she was embarrassed to be seen with me.

Three houses up the street, I saw Sandy, Maggy, and Ginny sitting on Sandy's sidewalk playing jacks.

"Who are they?" Sara asked.

"The teen queens," I said, wishing I had noticed them in time to lead Sara in the opposite direction.

"What do you mean?" Sara stared at me, her face expressionless.

"Oh, you know. They never do anything except sit around listening to records and talking about boys. They even wear green eye shadow." I looked down at my bare feet. "They hate me," I told my toes. "And I hate them."

Sara exhaled noisily and scowled. "I know the type. Creeps, real creeps," she said. "They'll hate me, too, and I'll hate them. It's always that way. But I could care less. Come on, introduce me."

Feeling a little better, I pedaled slowly toward the jacks game. By this time, Sandy, Ginny, and Maggy had noticed us. They shoved each other and Sandy said something in a low voice that made Ginny giggle. Maggy was the only one who smiled as we stopped our bikes next to them.

"Hi, Emily," Maggy said, but she, like Sandy and Ginny, was staring at Sara.

Flicking a braid over her shoulder, Sara stared back, squinting down at them as if they were amoebas squirming around in a drop of water under a microscope.

"This is Sara Slater," I said nervously. "Maggy, Sandy, Ginny." I pointed to each, wondering how people ever learned social graces.

"Hi," they said.

"Hi," Sara said.

There was a long silence. I was just about to say something clever about the heat when Maggy saved me from making a complete fool of myself by asking Sara if she was really from New York.

Sara nodded, staring at Maggy as if she were the most boring person she had ever met.

"Well, how do you like it here?" Maggy went on when Sara didn't say anything.

"I don't," Sara said without changing the expression on her face.

Maggy looked at Sandy and Ginny as if she expected them to say something, but Ginny just sat there bouncing her little red ball. From the expression on her face I could tell that she hated Sara already.

I looked at Sandy, wondering why she'd been quiet for so long. It wasn't like her to let an opportunity to say something nasty go by. Widening her eyes, she stared up at Sara with a little smile on her face. "You probably miss the sky-scrapers," she said softly. "I mean, they must have been the only things taller than you," she added, still smiling.

Instead of falling apart the way I would have, Sara smiled back at Sandy. Slowly she stretched out her foot and scattered Sandy's jacks into the grass, mashing a few of them in the process. "In New York," she said in a little soft breathy voice just like Sandy's, "nobody over seven plays jacks." She opened her eyes very wide. "Not unless they're retarded," she added.

Without saying another word, Sara turned her back on Sandy. "Come on, Em," she said and pedaled away.

As we turned the corner, I looked over my shoulder. Sandy, Ginny, and Maggy were down on their knees looking for the jacks. I smiled at Sara and she smiled back. I felt terrific. For once I hoped my mother was right, and that Sara would be an influence on me. Then I'd be able to say nasty things to Sandy and put Jamie in his place and tell my parents I was old enough to read any book I wanted to.

Maybe I'd even be able to persuade them to get me a ten-speed bike, just like Sara's.

FIVE

For the next week or so, Sara and I rode our bikes all over College Hills and lounged around each other's houses in the afternoons when it was too hot to do anything outside. I was happier than I'd been for a long time, and, even though I could tell that Mother wasn't exactly crazy about Sara, she was glad that I had someone to fool around with.

Once I even heard her tell Mrs. Rhodes that Sara was very bright. Intelligence is not the sort of thing that usually interests Mother or Mrs. Rhodes, but I think it was the only thing about Sara that Mother could find to compliment. After all, she didn't want Mrs. Rhodes to think that I had taken up with a complete zero when Maggy was so thick with Sandy, the number one dream daughter.

One hot afternoon, Sara and I were eating sandwiches under the cherry tree in our backyard, partly because it was cooler outside than it was inside and partly because Hairball and Jamie were having their lunch in the kitchen. It was the third day in a row that Sara and Hairball had managed to invite themselves in for lunch, and I had a feeling that Mother was getting a little annoyed about it.

"Brothers and sisters sure are a pain in the you-know-what, aren't they?" I asked. When Sara and I had gone out the back door, Jamie and Hairball had been blowing bubbles in their Kool-Aid and doing disgusting things with their peanut butter and jelly sandwiches.

Brushing a fly from her sandwich, Sara said, "You just haven't got Jamie trained, that's all. Hairball knows better than to give me any trouble."

I laughed, remembering how Sara had sent Hairball running home yesterday just by muttering something about a rat-faced boy. The things she said to Hairball were so funny they cracked me up.

"Want to know why Hairball behaves herself? It's because she knows the old gypsy woman will come and get her if she doesn't."

I stared at Sara. "What old gypsy woman?"

"Hairball's real mother, the one who left her on our doorstep when Hairball was a baby."

"What are you talking about?" I asked her, getting ready for a good laugh.

"It happened when I was six years old." Sara

paused and looked around, then leaned closer to me. "It was a dark and stormy night," she said dramatically, "and the howling of the wind kept me awake. I heard a rattling, banging sound, and at first I thought it was a limb hitting my window. But it kept getting louder and louder, so I got up and looked outside.

"At first I couldn't see anything, you know? But when my eyes got accustomed to the darkness, I saw an old woman, all ragged and dirty, pounding on the door. At her feet was a basket, and a sudden flash of lightning revealed its contents—a hideous baby screaming and crying."

Even though it was hot under the cherry tree, I shivered.

"The old woman was kicking the basket and cursing the baby while she banged on the door," Sara went on. "Finally the door opened and the old gypsy shoved the basket inside and ran away, shrieking with laughter. The baby, as you might have guessed, was Hairball." Sara sat back and swallowed a mouthful of cherry Kool-Aid.

I stared at her for a minute, wondering what the joke was. Surely she didn't expect me to believe a story like that. I mean, I wasn't Hairball. So I laughed. "Things like that don't happen in real life," I sputtered, choking on my drink.

"In New York, anything can happen." Sara

swirled her empty glass and tipped an ice cube into her mouth. Between grinding crunches, she continued, "My mother, of course, tells Hairball she's her real daughter, but I know the truth. And so does Hairball."

"Don't tell me Hairball remembers," I snorted.

"I've helped her to. After all, she has to be prepared for the day they come to get her, doesn't she?"

"They?"

"Sure. The old gypsy woman and her accomplice, Rick-the-Rat-faced-Boy. They spy on Hairball all the time, you know. She never would go down the sliding board in Central Park after I told her they used to hide under it just waiting for the right time to catch her and run away with her. And she still gets nervous in grocery stores because I often see them lurking behind the canned foods hoping to snatch her as she goes by. You should have seen her the time I told her I'd seen the old gypsy sitting at the foot of her bed watching her while she slept. Mom and Dad still can't figure out why she always wants to sleep in their bed."

"She doesn't really believe it, though, does she? I mean, she must know you're kidding her, right?"

"Of course she believes it. Why would I make up something like that?" Sara crunched another ice cube. "Do you have any cookies?" she asked.

I went inside and got four Oreos. Jamie and Hairball

were still giggling at the kitchen table and Mother gave me a look that said plainly she couldn't take much more of the Slaters. I pretended not to notice and went back outside, being careful not to let the screen door slam. There wasn't any sense in making Mother's mood even worse.

"What do you want to do now?" I asked Sara after we'd finished the cookies.

"How about a game of checkers?"

Reluctantly I went back inside and got the checkers. I'm very bad at games that require any thought. I guess I just can't take them seriously. That's why I like Parcheesi. In that game everybody is equal. You can toss the dice and move your men around the board and act silly and think about other stuff. Then, if you lose, it isn't because you were dumber than the other person. You just weren't as lucky.

As soon as Sara made her first move, I knew I was in trouble. Unlike me, she was very serious, and she thought a long time about every move. Even when she finally moved one of her men, she didn't take her hand off right away but sat there a little longer wondering if she'd done the right thing. Actually, she never had a thing to worry about. She won every game easily.

But what really upset me was her attitude. "That was a dumb move," she'd say after I'd taken my turn; then she'd triple-jump me. "Don't you ever think ahead?'' she'd ask after double-jumping the two kings I'd worked so hard to get. I kept on laughing and doing dumb things on purpose so I could tell myself I hadn't really tried to win. But all the time, I was afraid I was going to cry because Sara made me feel like such a stupid person.

Around four o'clock I heard Sara's mother calling her and Hairball. I felt the way a prizefighter must feel when he's losing and he hears the bell ring and he knows his partner is going to stop hitting him.

''Now what could she want?'' Sara got up and stretched. ''Usually the longer we're gone, the happier she is.''

''What does your mother do all day anyway?'' Although I knew her mother didn't work, it puzzled me that I hardly ever saw her. She was always busy upstairs, but unlike my mother, it wasn't housework she was doing up there. I mean, the entire house was a wreck and they'd only lived in it for a few weeks.

''Didn't I tell you?'' Sara yawned widely, displaying a mouthful of fillings, and scratched her head. ''She's writing a novel.''

''Really?'' I was truly impressed. A writer living right across the street from me. No wonder she never bothered to do dull, everyday things like housework. ''I've never met a writer, Sara.''

''Mom's not officially a writer,'' Sara said. ''I

mean, she hasn't found a publisher yet for any of her stuff."

I tried to hide my disappointment. I'd been all ready to ask for an autographed copy of her latest book. "What kind of a book is she trying to write?"

"Well, she started to write a sex novel, but she got so embarrassed she couldn't finish it. Then she started a historical romance, but she got bored doing research. Now she's working on a mystery about an old lady who lives in a nursing home and pays her hospital bills by robbing banks. She says it's got social significance, but she can't figure out how to end it."

"It sounds good," I said.

"She's having a lot of trouble with it," Sara said. "Sometimes I think the best thing that could happen would be for Frank to eat the manuscript. Then maybe Mom would pay some attention to what's going on in the world instead of locking herself up in her study and banging away on a typewriter all day and yelling at everybody who interrupts her."

Mother poked her head out the back door. "Sara, your mother has been calling you for five minutes. Don't you think you ought to find out what she wants?"

As soon as Sara left, Mother came outside and sat down beside me on the grass. Just as I thought, she got right to the point.

"Doesn't Mrs. Slater ever fix meals for Sara and

Jennifer?'' she asked. ''Doesn't she wonder where they are all day?''

''Oh, Sara tells her they're coming over here, so she doesn't have to worry. Anyway, she's busy writing a book,'' I said, wishing Mother did something more creative than stitching up needlework kits.

''At this point, I wouldn't care if she were Virginia Woolf, Gertrude Stein, and Daphne du Maurier all rolled up into one,'' Mother said. ''I'm not going to have those kids hanging around my house all day going through food like a plague of locusts.''

She held up a pack of Oreo cookies with three left in it. ''This morning this package hadn't even been opened and now look at it. Almost empty. I can't afford this, especially when it's never reciprocated. Three days in a row they've had lunch here this week, and a couple of days last week. It has to stop, Emily. Do you understand?''

''We certainly didn't eat all those cookies,'' I said indignantly. ''Jamie and Hairball must have been in them.''

''Emily, don't talk back! Just see to it that you understand that having lunch does not include Sara and Hair-I mean Jennifer.'' She got up and walked back across the grass, tugging her shorts down. ''Come inside now and help with dinner.''

Muttering Sara-type things under my breath, I followed her inside.

SIX

For the next week, it rained every day and Sara and I almost went crazy with boredom.

Whenever Mother would let me, I went over to Sara's house because nobody cared what we did over there. Unlike my mother, Mrs. Slater didn't have a long list of rules fastened to the refrigerator door with a magnet. We could eat in the living room and put glasses down on tables without worrying about leaving rings. We could shout and run around the house. We could turn the record player on as loud as we wanted to. We could jump on the beds and play hide-and-seek in every room but Mrs. Slater's study and have water fights in the rain without cleaning up the mud we tracked in afterward. In fact, we could do anything we wanted as long as we didn't open the study door and disturb the clickety-clack of the typewriter.

Of course, there was one problem at Sara's. Hairball. Unlike Jamie, who was always being shipped off to a friend's house for the afternoon, Hairball spent her days at home, crouched in front of the TV stroking this awful purple rabbit she carries everywhere and sucking her thumb. She really got on Sara's and my nerves, so we livened up some of our afternoons by dreaming up tricks to play on her.

Sometimes we told her scary stories about the crazy old woman Sara swore lived up in the attic, and sometimes we pretended to see the old gypsy woman peeping in the window. When we weren't in the mood for making up stories, Sara would grab Hairball's rabbit and we'd play a game of keep-away with it or hide it in the basement or the attic, two places Hairball was scared to go by herself. Once we put blue food coloring in a glass of milk and made her drink it, even though it almost made her throw up.

To tell you the truth, every once in a while our teasing Hairball bothered me a little bit, but she was Sara's sister and if Sara thought what we were doing was okay, who was I to argue? After all, we never physically hurt Hairball. I'd have drawn the line there. And, as Sara said, a little teasing never hurt anybody. If anything, it toughened them up. Take me, for instance. If I'd had a big sister like Sara to get me in shape, I'd have been ready for Sandy. Nothing she said would ever have upset me if I'd been used to that kind of stuff.

One particularly damp and gloomy afternoon, the three of us were sitting in Sara's living room. As usual, Hairball was watching cartoons on television. One of Sara's cats was sitting in between pots of half-dead plants on the windowsill and staring at the raindrops running down the glass. On the floor were the checkers (Sara had beaten me three times and then gotten bored), a huge pile of comic books, plates with the crusts of sandwiches on them, empty glasses, a half-dressed Barbie doll with most of its hair cut off, a pack of cards, a tennis shoe, a pink sock, yesterday's newspaper, and an overturned plant. I was sprawled on the end of my spine reading *The Bloodville Horror*.

Suddenly Sara kicked the comic books across the floor and jumped up.

"What's the matter?" I asked, hoping Sara hadn't noticed that I'd nearly jumped out of my skin.

"Let's make cookies," she said. "Come on, Em."

Although I was in the middle of one of the most terrifying scenes in the book, I was happy to put it down and follow Sara out of the living room.

As usual, the kitchen looked like an army had just marched through it. A pot full of burned spaghetti and cloudy water was sitting in the sink along with half a dozen dirty glasses, a stack of greasy plates and bowls, and three or four coffee mugs. More dirty dishes and silverkware flowed out of the sink and across the counter.

44

Shoving dishes and cereal boxes out of the way, Sara started collecting the ingredients we needed. When she had everything, she handed me a measuring cup and we got busy. I'd never been allowed to do anything in our kitchen without Mother hanging over my shoulder and telling me not to get flour on the floor, and warning me that I'd get worms from eating raw dough, and nagging me to clean up when I was finished, so I had a great time. If Sara didn't mind the mess, why should I? Nothing we did could possibly make the kitchen look worse than it had when we started.

When we had spooned nearly all of the batter onto the cookie sheets, Sara grabbed the bowl.

"Hold everything, Em," she said. Before I knew what she was doing, she had picked up a box of detergent and sprinkled some of it into the batter at the bottom of the bowl. "Don't worry, this isn't for you, Em," she said. "It's for Hairball. Don't you think she needs a little lesson in manners?"

"What do you mean?"

"You'll see." With great care, Sara shaped the soapy batter into a big cookie and put it on a baking sheet all by itself.

"You're not going to make her eat it, are you? She'll get sick, Sara." Uncomfortably I realized that we were about to cross the no-physical-injury line I'd drawn.

45

"Of course I'm going to offer it to her. If she takes it, it's her fault."

"She'll never eat it, she's not that dumb." I watched Sara shove the baking sheet into the oven.

"You don't know Hairball like I know Hairball," Sara said. "She's such a pig, the minute she sees how big that cookie is, she'll want it."

I stood there nibbling on one of the cookies from the first batch and wondering if I should try to talk Sara out of giving the cookie to Hairball. I had a feeling she'd call me a goody-goody if I told her what I was thinking, so I convinced myself that soap couldn't hurt anyone.

When the cookie was done, Sara put it on a plate with a bunch of burned ones. It looked a little foamy, so she wiped it off and carried the plate into the living room.

"See what we made, Hairball," Sara said. "Would you like one?"

Hairball looked so pleased I felt sorry for her. Sara didn't usually let her have anything we made unless the poor kid said and did all sorts of things to earn it. And even then, about all she ever got was the old burned kernels at the bottom of the popcorn bowl or something equally delicious.

"Oh, Sara, they look good," she said and reached up toward the plate, hesitating a little as if she feared Sara might snatch it away. "Can I have any one I want?'' Her hand hovered over the big one.

Sara nodded. ''Any one you like.'' She held the plate so close to Hairball I was afraid she'd smell the soap.

''Even this one?'' Hairball pointed at the big one.

''Even that one.'' Sara winked at me and I tried hard not to laugh. As mean as Sara was, I couldn't help thinking she was funny.

''Maybe I shouldn't, though. It's the biggest one.'' Hairball looked worriedly back and forth from Sara to me. I had to turn away to keep from laughing, but Sara kept her face a perfect blank.

''It's all right, Hairball,'' she said.

''Are you sure?''

''Yes, I'm sure. Go on and take it.'' A little edge was creeping into Sara's voice, and I knew she was going to get mad if Hairball kept on stalling.

Like a little cat, Hairball finally reached out and grabbed the cookie. Opening her mouth wide, she took a big bite. Almost at once her face turned red and she gagged and spit foamy cookie dough all over the place. With froth around her mouth, she jumped up and ran out to the kitchen, leaving her rabbit in a heap on the floor.

Sara followed her out of the room, and I heard her say, ''What's the matter, Hairball? Didn't you like the cookie I made for you?''

Hairball responded with some wordless gurgling sounds.

"Want some more?" Sara asked.

"No! No!"

"No, *thank you*, Hairball, is what you should say, and that is your second free lesson in manners for today. The first was never take the biggest cookie on the plate—even if someone offers it to you." Sara laughed and came back into the living room with the rest of the cookies.

"Oh, good, it's Daffy Duck," she said, plopping down in front of the television set and putting the plate of cookies between us.

While Sara sat there laughing and stuffing cookies into her mouth, I could hear Hairball crying out in the kitchen.

"Do you think she's all right?" I asked Sara.

"Who?"

"Hairball. She's still crying. Maybe we should go see if she's okay."

"Don't worry about her. She's just a crybaby." Sara stuck another cookie in her mouth.

"Doesn't your mother ever get mad at you for teasing Hairball?" I asked, wishing Sara would close her mouth when she chewed.

Sara shrugged. "She never cares what I do as long as I don't disturb her. What's it to you anyway?"

"I just wondered, that's all. I mean, my mother

48

would kill me if I ever treated Jamie like that.''

Sara didn't say anything, so I sat beside her watching Daffy Duck doing terrible things to Elmer Fudd. Every now and then I glanced at Sara's profile, but she never took her eyes off of the television screen. I wanted to ask her if she was mad at me, but I couldn't. For one thing, I knew I'd whine if I did, and she hates whining. For another, I was pretty sure she'd say yes, she was mad, and then what would I say?

Finally I got up and looked out the window. It was still raining, of course. ''Listen, I have to go,'' I said. ''It must be almost time for dinner.''

Sara didn't take her eyes off Daffy Duck. ''Sure, see you later,'' she said.

I stood in the living room doorway for a few seconds, wishing she'd at least look at me, but she didn't. I could see Hairball sitting on the steps sucking her thumb and petting one of the cats. She didn't look at me either.

''Well, good-bye,'' I said.

''Bye.''

Feeling kind of depressed, I left Sara's house and started across the street. Walking toward Maggy's house were Sandy, Ginny, and Maggy. They all had umbrellas, and Sandy and Ginny were lugging sleeping bags and overnight cases. Hoping they wouldn't notice me, I looked the other way and pretended not to see them. What did I care if Maggy was having a slumber party?

"Roses are red!" Sandy yelled.

"Violets are blue!" Ginny added.

"A giraffe like you belongs in the zoo!" all three of them shouted.

Pretending to be deaf as well as blind, I kept walking, splashing through the puddles and wishing every sheet of water I kicked in the air were a tidal wave sweeping them out to sea.

"Hey, can't you say anything?" Ginny shrieked.

"Fool, of course she can't," Sandy said. "Giraffes can't make a sound. Their necks are too long."

"Oh, of course, how foolish of me." Ginny giggled.

"But they sure can run!" Sandy added as I dashed up the sidewalk and into my house.

Mother looked up from the pile of laundry she was sorting, surprised to see me home so early. "What was all that shouting outside?" she asked, getting up and looking out the window just in time to see Sandy and Ginny stagger up the Rhodeses' front steps and vanish inside with their sleeping bags.

"Maggy must be having a little slumber party," she said. "It's a shame the way you've turned your back on your old friends since Sara moved in, Emily. You and Maggy used to have so much fun together. I just don't understand how you can drop her this way. And that darling Sandy Smith. What's so fascinating about Sara I just don't know.''

Before she could say anything else, I ran up to my bedroom and slammed the door behind me. How could my own mother be so blind? Didn't she understand anything?

SEVEN

That evening I was sprawled on the couch watching a dumb TV show because I was too hot to do anything else. I heard the phone ring, but I let Mother answer it. I was sure it was Sara calling to apologize for being so rude, and I didn't want her to think I was sitting by the phone waiting for her to call me.

But Mother talked for a while and then came to the living-room door. "It's for you, Emily. It's Mrs. Barnett," she said, smiling at me.

Wondering what on earth Ginny's mother could possibly want to talk to me about, I walked slowly out into the hall and picked up the receiver. "Hello?"

"Hello, Emily. How are you?" Mrs. Barnett asked.

"Fine," I whispered.

"Good. I'm calling you about the party Ginny's having a week from Saturday. It's nothing fancy, just dinner and maybe some dancing afterward. We wanted to get the whole seventh grade together before school starts to celebrate the end of summer. Can you come?"

"I guess so." I immediately hated myself for not being able to think of an excuse fast enough.

"Well, that's wonderful, Emily. We'll look forward to seeing you, dear. One more thing before I let you go, though. Can you give me Sara Slater's number so I can call her, too? I don't want to leave anyone out."

Feeling like a traitor, I gave her Sara's number. After all, if I had to go, Sara should, too. It was only fair.

"Well, good-bye, Emily. See you next week," Mrs. Barnett said in the high, phony-sounding voice she uses frequently, especially when she talks to kids.

"Good-bye." I sat there staring at the receiver until I heard the beep beep beep that warns you that your phone is off the hook. Then I slowly lowered it, wondering why Mrs. Barnett wanted Sara and me to come to Ginny's party. Surely Ginny didn't want us there. Maybe she had only called to be polite, maybe she had expected me to say no. My face flushed. Of course, that was it. I was supposed to say no.

As I sat there, staring at the phone and trying to get the nerve to call Mrs. Barnett and tell her I couldn't come, Mother appeared with a big smile on her face. "Did you say yes?" she asked.

53

I nodded. "But I'm going to call Mrs. Barnett and tell her I made a mistake."

"A mistake? Oh, Emily, don't be silly. Of course you're not going to call and say something like that. The party is a perfect way for you and Sara to become part of the gang again. All you girls need is a chance to know each other better."

"You mean you already knew about this and you really expect me to go?" I leaped up from the chair.

"Emily, lower your voice! You'll wake up Jamie," Mother said. "Certainly you're going."

"I won't go, you can't make me, you can't. Don't you understand? They all hate me, they really do. They don't want Sara and me there. They already know us as well as they want to. Please don't make me go, please!"

"Emily, don't make a scene. You're going to Ginny's party and that's that. If you want to discuss it in the morning, fine, but I think you should go to your room now. I can't stand these outbursts. I'm getting a headache."

I left her in the hall and ran upstairs to my room. With my door closed, I undressed in the dark, hurling my clothes to the floor as I took them off. I didn't want to cry again. After all, I wasn't Hairball, was I? But I couldn't help it. It seemed to me that all my life my mother had been calling the things that hurt me the most "silly." The only times I ever got any sympathy from her were when I was sick or bleeding. To convince her I was hurt, I had to produce a fever, a bruise, a cut, or a broken bone. Like Maggy on the day of the Valentine party, she would consider being called a giraffe a joke and tell me to laugh it off. Some joke.

Burying my face in my pillow, I wept until my pillowcase was wet. Then I turned it over and tried to go to sleep, but my room was hot and stuffy. Strange shadows moved in the corners, my venetian blind rattled every now and then when a puff of warm wind came through the window, and, over the roar of the Rhodeses' air conditioner, I could hear Maggy and her guests shrieking and singing along with the record player. Lying there watching the headlights from passing cars skim across my ceiling, I felt very lonesome.

The morning sun was hot when I woke up, and I got out of bed slowly, wishing that summer were over. When fall came, Ginny's party would merely be another horrible memory instead of a monster lurking just over the horizon.

I got dressed and spent half an hour braiding my hair. When I was finished, it didn't look very nice, not at all like Sara's. My hair wasn't really long enough or thick enough or straight enough to make good-looking braids. Little pieces wisped out here and there, my part was crooked, and one braid looked longer than the other. But I felt cooler with my hair off my neck, so I went downstairs hoping Sara wouldn't think I was copying her when she saw me.

When I walked into the kitchen, I saw Mother already hard at work cleaning the refrigerator.

"It's about time you got up," she said, her back to me.

As I brushed past her to get the milk, she noticed my braids. "What have you done to your hair?" she asked.

"Braided it." I poured milk into a bowl of Rice Krispies, listening to their familiar chorus of snap, crackle, and pop. "You're always saying I should do something with it, so I did."

"That certainly isn't what I had in mind. It looks absolutely awful, and so do your clothes. They're wrinkled and dirty. You look more and more like Sara Slater every day. You walk like her, you talk like her, you dress like her. For heaven's sake, Emily, if you have to have someone to imitate, pick a girl like Sandy Smith. I can't stand seeing you follow Sara around like some kind of a maid!"

I slammed down my spoon on the table. "I don't follow Sara around, but I'd rather look like her than Sandy! I hate Sandy, and if you knew what she's really like, you'd hate her too!"

"Emily, don't raise your voice to me! I won't tolerate it! Just because the Slaters let Sara yell at them doesn't mean you can get away with it."

"You hate me, don't you? You want a daughter like Sandy, that's what you want, isn't it? Well, I'm not like her and I never will be!"

"Stop it, Emily! I will not talk to you until you calm down!" Turning her back, Mother started yanking things out of the freezer.

"You don't want to talk about it because you know it's true!" I screamed. "But I don't care, I don't care!" Dumping my untouched cereal in the sink, I ran out the back door, letting it slam behind me. With my back to the house, I sat down on the swing set and started to sob.

After I'd sat there for at least five minutes, I heard someone come down the back steps. Thinking it might be Mother coming to apologize, I wiped my eyes and nose.

"Emily?"

Startled, I turned around and tried to smile at Sara. I hoped she wouldn't notice I'd been crying.

"Your mother definitely hates me," she said, sitting down on the other swing. "When I came to the door, she just mumbled something and walked away."

"It's not you she hates, it's me. We just had a horrible fight. She, she—" I stopped, unable to go on. Already my chin was wobbling and I could feel tears filling up my eyes.

"So? I fight with my mother all the time. It's no big deal, Em. It's a perfectly normal adolescent thing.'' She rocked her swing back and forth. ''What did you fight about? No, no, let me guess. Did it have anything to do with a certain girl who just happens to be having a sweet little back-to-school party?''

I nodded. ''Did Mrs. Barnett call you?''

''Yep.''

I waited for her to continue. When she didn't, I said, ''Well? You don't have to go, do you?''

She stared at her feet. ''As a matter of fact, I do.''

''How come? I was kind of hoping your mother would think it was a dumb idea and maybe talk my mother into letting me stay at home.''

''Well, Mrs. Barnett picked a bad time to call. Mom was in a terrible mood because her book isn't working out right and Dad's been nagging her about spending so much time writing. I think he's tired of having dried-up hamburgers for dinner, you know? So last night he started yelling at her about me growing up without any manners, and when Mrs. Barnett called to ask me to go to the party, Dad told her I'd be glad to go, and that was that. All the arguing in the world isn't going to change his mind.''

We sat there on the swings for a while without saying anything. As disappointed as I was in Sara's mother and father, I was glad that Sara seemed to have gotten over being mad at me. So, even though I would have liked to ask her if Hairball was all right, not sick or anything from the cookie, I decided not to mention it. It was better to have a friend than to risk making Sara mad at me again.

"Come on," Sara said at last. "We can't sit around here feeling sorry for ourselves all day. Let's do something."

Although I hoped she wasn't going to suggest a game of checkers, I was prepared to do anything she wanted. I got up and followed her around our house and down to the end of our street. Stopping in the shade of a tree, Sara smiled at me.

"Want a cigarette?"

I stared at her as she took a pack of Marlboros out of her Girl Scout shirt pocket. "I didn't know you smoked," I said.

"Are you shocked?"

"Of course not," I lied.

"Do you want one, or are you too goody-goody?" Sara held the pack under my nose.

"Suppose somebody drives past and sees us?" I stalled.

Sara shrugged. "Where's a good place?"

I pointed across the street. "How about down there?"

"On the railroad tracks?"

"Sure. Nobody can see us from the road and if a train comes we'll hear it when it's miles away."

We crossed the street and pushed through the tall grass growing on the top of the bank. Below us, the tracks shimmered in the hot sunlight. We slid down the cindery banks and walked along the ties until Sara thought we were fairly invisible to anyone driving above us.

Since there wasn't anyplace else to sit, we squatted down on a track that was so hot I could feel it right through the seat of my shorts. Sara held out the pack again and I took one.

"Have you ever smoked before?" Sara asked, putting her cigarette in her mouth and lighting it.

"Oh, sure," I said, taking the matches and trying to light mine exactly the way she had. It tasted even worse than I expected it to, and I spit it out, coughing and choking.

"Emily, you lit the filter!" Sara shouted. Handing me another cigarette, she said, "This end is supposed to go in your mouth, stupid."

"I know, I just made a mistake," I said. Hoping it would taste better this time, I lit the cigarette cautiously. Actually it didn't seem any different at all, but I puffed on it anyway.

"I used to smoke all the time in New York," Sara said, coughing a couple of times. "Everybody did. Kids up there are a lot more sophisticated, you know? I'll bet Sandy never even tried it."

"Not her. Not Maggy or Ginny either."

We sat there, the sun beating down on us, coughing every now and then and congratulating ourselves for being a lot more daring than anyone else we knew. The only bad thing about it was how terrible it tasted and how much it hurt my throat. It was hard to believe that anybody really enjoyed smoking.

Watching Sara light up another one, I started thinking about the Indians. How had they ever thought of smoking? I mean, can you imagine being the first person to roll up some dead, ground-up leaves in a piece of paper or a leaf or whatever they used, lighting them, and breathing the smoke into your lungs? What kind of a person comes up with a weird idea like that?

Luckily for me, there were only four cigarettes in the pack, so after Sara finished her second one, she coughed a few times and got up. "What's that thing for?" She pointed at a small cinder-block bunker built into the side of the railroad bank.

"I don't know. It's always been there. I think railroad repair crews used to store their tools in it or something. Nobody uses it now."

Sara climbed up the bank and stepped onto the bunker's flat tin roof. Seeing a trapdoor, she bent down and struggled to lift it. When she finally got it open, she knelt down and looked inside. "It smells awful down there," she said.

I climbed onto the roof next to her. "I think boys use it for a latrine or something," I said. "Any rain gets in, so it's always damp and smelly." When I was little, I used to have nightmares about being trapped down there in the smelly dark with spiders and snakes crawling all over me.

"Have you ever gone down the ladder?"

I shook my head. "Too smelly. Once I looked down there and saw a dead chicken with its head torn off. It was all bloody, and its feathers were scattered all over the place."

Sara lowered herself over the edge and climbed inside. I peered down at her.

"No dead chicken down here now," she said. "But it sure does stink. Come on down, Em, there's dirty words and pictures and stuff all over the walls. A bunch of perverts must live around here. It's worse than the New York subway."

Feeling kind of sick from the taste the cigarette had left in my mouth, I climbed slowly down the ladder. Sara was right. Down here the stench of urine and cinders and something worse was almost unbearable.

"Look." Sara lit a match and held it up to the wall. "I sure wish we had a can of spray paint."

Squinting at the wall, I noticed Froggy's name. When I looked closer, I saw something pretty awful about Ginny. I pointed it out to Sara. "Do you think it's true?"

"I'd believe anything about Ginny," Sara said. She

lit another match and prowled around, examining one message after another. "I don't see your name anywhere, Em, but there's plenty of stuff about Sandy and Maggy."

"I know." I was glad it was dark, because I was sure my face was purple. Maybe it wasn't so bad to be tall and skinny after all. "It looks mostly like Froggy and Jeff's writing, which isn't too surprising because they're the biggest perverts in College Hills. I can just see them down here in the dark writing dirty things on the walls. Like slugs or something."

"Let's get some fresh air," Sara said, and I followed her up the ladder gratefully.

"You know," Sara said, looking back down inside the bunker, "that's the perfect place for the old gypsy and Rick-the-Rat-faced-Boy to hang out. I can just see them down there drinking wine and writing on the walls and waiting for Hairball. Can't you, Em?"

I nodded. By this time the old gypsy and the rat-faced boy were almost as real to me as they were to Hairball. I could imagine them crouching in the dark, ripping heads off chickens and scattering their feathers around like snow.

"Well, thanks for showing me the bunker, Em. It's a great place to cool off on a hot day." She jumped off the roof with her braids swinging. "Come on, let's

63

go back to my house and have a Coke. It's so hot in this state, I can't stand it.''

I jumped off right behind her, thinking that a nice cold drink just might wash the taste of tobacco out of my mouth.

EIGHT

A few days later, Sara and I were lying on her bedroom floor reading comic books. Suddenly Sara sighed loudly and tossed *Wonder Woman* across the room.

"Why can't anything exciting ever happen around here? I'm so bored I could die. There's nothing to do here, nothing at all."

"I know," I said.

"What do you think Sandy and her slaves do all day?"

"Oh, sit around and swoon over rock stars and talk about boys and read Ginny's sex education books. Exciting stuff like that."

"Ginny would have sex education books. She's just the type." Sara picked up another comic book and fanned herself with it. "I saw Maggy go over to Ginny's a little while ago. Why don't we walk past her house and see what they're doing?"

65

Since I couldn't think of anything else to do, I followed Sara outside. We didn't see Maggy, Ginny, or Sandy, but we did see Mrs. Barnett sitting on her front steps reading the afternoon paper. She smiled pleasantly and waved at us.

"Are you looking for the girls? They're down in the recreation room practicing dancing, and I'm sure they'd be happy to see you two," Mrs. Barnett said, apparently oblivious of her daughter's feelings about Sara and me. That's the kind of mother she is. Always thinking everything is fine, no matter how much evidence there is to the contrary.

Sara smiled sweetly. "Thank you, but we're on our way to the store. Mom's out of milk." She spoke so politely I could hardly keep a straight face.

As soon as we were around the corner, Sara spun around a couple of times and wiggled her hips.

"I already know all there is to know about dancing," she said, and twirled around again, banging me with her hips and sending me flying into the Morgans' hedge. "That's a new step. You use it when you want to get rid of your partner."

I untangled myself from the hedge, but Sara gave me another shove and I fell through into the Morgans' yard.

Before I could get up, Sara crashed through the hedge after me. "Come on, we'll cut through the Morgans' yard to Ginny's yard and look in the window. Can't you just see Ginny dancing? Imagine all that blubber bouncing around! It ought to be a riot.''

Sara darted across the yard, threading her way through an obstacle course of lawn chairs, with me panting at her heels. With ease, she vaulted over a chain link fence between the Barnetts' and the Morgans' yards, and I followed more slowly, scared of cutting myself on the wire edges. Safely behind the Barnetts' garage, we stared at the broad expanse of sunny lawn stretching between us and the shrubbery screening the basement windows.

"Do you see anyone?" Sara squinted at the house.

Examining each window for a frowning face about to yell at us, I shook my head.

"Okay, follow me."

We raced to the bushes and ducked under them, trying not to make any noise. Our only witness was the Barnetts' fat Persian cat, napping on the cool ground between the house and the bushes. Giving us a nasty look that reminded me of Ginny, he slunk away, leaving his resting place to us. We wedged ourselves between a bush covered with sharp thorns and the garden hose coiled on the ground by the spigot.

Through the open window, we heard Maggy say, "Put on a fast one next. I'm sick of all this slow stuff."

"After this one," Ginny said.

"That's what you said last time," Maggy shouted, to make herself heard above the record player.

"It's my house and my record player and my records, so we'll hear what I want to hear," Ginny shouted back.

"What's the matter, Ginny? Can't you move fast enough for the good ones?" Sandy asked.

By now, Sara and I had edged our way to the window. We could see Maggy and Ginny standing by the record player, their backs to us, but we couldn't see Sandy.

"Maybe she just wants to pretend she's dancing with Jeff," Maggy said sarcastically.

"Oh, shut up!" Ginny shouted.

"Don't start that stuff about Jeff again. I'm so sick of hearing about Jeff, I could puke at the mere mention of his name. He's nothing compared to Bruce." Sandy came spinning up to the record player. She was hugging a pillow, and her hair swirled around her face like a shampoo commercial. "I'll bet he asks me to go with him at the party, don't you?"

Ginny and Maggy looked at her and rolled their eyes up at the ceiling.

"You don't have to be so conceited about it," Maggy said. "Just because he's always hanging around your house and all. The only reason he comes is to play basketball with your brothers. He's their friend, that's all."

"You sure aren't jealous or anything, are you?" Sandy flipped her hair around just to make sure nobody had missed seeing how beautiful it was.

"Jealous?" Maggy snorted. "Of Bruce Benyon? You must be kidding."

"Oh, come on, don't fight," Ginny pleaded.

Just then, Mrs. Barnett appeared carrying a tray piled high with cookies and three glasses full of ice and Coke. As Maggy, Sandy, and Ginny pounced on the refreshments and started gorging themselves, Mrs. Barnett sat down on the couch and smiled at them. She acted as if she were hoping they would include her in the conversation, but nobody said anything interesting. In fact, they seemed to ignore her. After a few minutes, she excused herself and went back upstairs.

As soon as she was gone, they started talking about boys again.

"Froggy is so disgusting," Maggy said. "Why did you invite him?"

"I told you. Mother made me invite everybody."

"But the way his eyes pop out. I won't be able to eat if I have to sit near him."

"Just don't dance with him. He'll try to feel you," Sandy added.

"And what about Tommy Lawson and the way he spits all over you when he talks?" Ginny said after they'd stopped shrieking about Froggy. "Tommy's such a jerk. Always following Froggy around and try-ing to act tough.''

While Sara and I listened, the three of them dis-cussed every boy in our class. Bruce, Jeff, and Steve Sunderland were the only ones they didn't have some-thing nasty to say about. By the time they'd finished with the last of the boys, they were laughing so hard they could hardly talk.

''What are we going to do with all those creeps?'' Maggy howled. ''Suppose they want to dance with us or something?''

''Why do you think we invited Giraffe Girl and Skyscraper?'' Sandy asked.

Feeling my face flush, I nudged Sara. ''Let's go,'' I whispered. I should have realized that sooner or later they would say something about Sara and me.

Sara shook her head and leaned a little closer to the window to hear what else they had to say.

''Can't you just see Sara and Froggy together?'' Ginny giggled.

''The perfect couple!'' Maggy laughed so hard she choked on her Coke and Sandy had to pound her on the back to make her stop coughing.

''She's so tall he'd only come to her stomach,'' Sandy said, laughing. ''Too bad she doesn't have any-thing up top for him to get fresh with!''

That was when Sara decided to take action. Before I knew what she was doing, she turned on the spigot, grabbed the hose, and pointed it toward the window. As soon as I saw the stream of water hit Sandy in the face, I jumped up and started backing out of the bushes, tripping and stumbling and probably sounding like a baby buffalo on the warpath.

As I retreated, I heard Sandy shriek and Sara say, in an unbelievably calm tone of voice, ''That should teach you not to talk about people behind their backs.''

Tossing the hose aside, Sara got up and walked away from the window, ignoring the shouts from the recreation room. ''Come on, Em,'' she said, strolling casually away from the house.

She didn't need to say it twice. I was so scared of getting bawled out by Mrs. Barnett that I was already several steps ahead of her.

''Slow down,'' she said. ''Be cool, Em.''

Thanks to her advice, we were barely out of the Barnetts' yard when Sandy came hurtling around the side of the house, her hair, face, and T-shirt dripping.

''Come back here, Sara Slater!'' she yelled.

Sara turned around, her arms folded across her chest, and stared coldly at Sandy, one eyebrow raised. ''Yes?''

At that, Sandy, with Maggy and Ginny flanking her, went into a screaming tirade. I looked at Sara, waiting for her to give me a cue. At first I thought she was just going to stand there sneering, but finally she lost her temper and started yelling insults. And I, of course, made the mistake of joining in.

NINE

Just as I called Sandy one of the worst names I know, my mother appeared out of nowhere. There I was, halfway between our house and the Barnetts' house, screaming obscenities at the top of my lungs, with Sara beside me shouting even louder. Sandy, of course, had seen Mother coming. She was standing in the middle of the street looking like a martyred Miss America with Ginny and Maggy on either side of her, her ladies-in-waiting. It was not a good scene.

"Emily Anne Sherwood!" Mother called. "Come home this minute!"

For a second I stood where I was, wondering how I was going to explain my behavior. Taking my hesitation as a sign of defiance, Mother strode up the street, closely followed by Jamie and Hairball, who looked like they'd spent the morning in a mud puddle.

Without saying a word, she grabbed my arm and yanked me toward our house.

"It was all their fault," Sara said helpfully. "You should have heard what Sandy called Emily, Mrs. Sherwood. It was ten times worse than anything Emily said."

"I don't care to discuss it, Sara," Mother said in a tight voice. "Please go home now and take your sister with you."

"But . . ." Sara started.

"Come inside, Emily. You too, Jamie," Mother said, not giving Sara a chance to say another word. I couldn't believe she was capable of being so rude to my friend.

Giving Sara an apologetic look, I followed Mother up the front steps and into the house. As soon as the door closed behind us, she launched into a terrible tirade about my behavior, blaming the whole scene on Sara and refusing to let me say a word in her defense. Finally she told me that I was to stay in the house for the rest of the day and in our yard for the rest of the week. I wasn't to talk to Sara, not even on the phone, until Ginny's party.

Knowing there was no appeal, I made my usual escape to my room and stayed there until Mother called me for dinner.

Talk about an unpleasant meal. For one thing, Mother had tried a receipe from one of her magazines, some awful thing made out of noodles and soup and tuna fish and nasty little red things. Neither Jamie nor I could do much more than pick at it, trying to eat the tuna fish and leave everything else.

And while we were sitting there lining the edges of our plates with the red things, we had to listen to Mother describe our behavior to Daddy. It seemed that while Sara and I had been squirting Sandy, Jamie had followed Hairball down to the park and played in the creek. Although I didn't see how he could have drowned in two inches of water, Mother was going on and on about it, insisting that it was all the Slaters' fault that these terrible things were happening.

Daddy kept mumbling little responses, but even I could see that he was more interested in the news. His eyes were fixed on the TV and he was listening to every word the reporter had to say about the kidnapping of a high government official in some country in South America. He obviously thought the terrorists' demands were a lot more important than Jamie's close brush with death in the creek and my disgraceful behavior in the street.

Finally Mother realized that Daddy wasn't listening, and she got mad at him. For a minute I thought they were going to have a real fight like the ones Sara says her parents have. I was hoping Mother would throw what was left of the casserole at Daddy, but he just got up and went into his den. He closed the door behind him, and in a few seconds I heard the newscaster start up in there. This time he was describing a plane crash in Japan. "No Americans were on board," I heard him say, as if it didn't matter that one hundred and thirteen other people had died.

Without Daddy there to get mad at, Mother started fussing at Jamie and me for not eating our dinner. She told us we couldn't have any dessert unless we ate everything on our plates, including the pimientos, which was what she called the red things. I left Jamie at the table crying as he poked food into his mouth. I was tired of ice cream anyway.

When I woke up the next morning, I was too depressed to get out of bed. I had no idea what I was going to do for the next five days. The thought of playing endless games of Candyland with Jamie did not excite me. Neither did reading or drawing or lying in the hammock.

By eleven o'clock it was too hot to stay in my room, so I dragged myself out of bed. Before I went downstairs, I braided my hair, daring Mother to say a word about it. After a solitary breakfast, I wandered into the living room and gazed out the window, wondering if Sara was as bored as I was.

As if to answer my question, she zoomed by our house on her ten-speed. She looked anything but bored. Why had I thought she was being punished too? I should have realized that Mrs. Slater wouldn't go to pieces over a few obscenities shouted in the street.

The days crept by, each one longer and hotter and more boring than the one before. Mother kept me busy helping her with things like scrubbing the floors and washing the windows and entertaining Jamie. Believe it or not, I actually spent an entire morning sitting in the sandbox helping Jamie build a superhighway system for a fleet of Tonka trucks. If Sara had seen me, I'd have died of embarrassment, but it was a whole lot better than helping Mother reorganize the kitchen cupboards.

One afternoon I was lying on the couch trying to get interested in a TV program when I heard Hairball screeching out in the street. Looking out the window, I saw Sara riding her bike in circles around Hairball. She was holding Hairball's old rabbit on the handlebars and Hairball was trying to get him.

"Give him to me! Give him to me!" Hairball shouted.

"He likes riding on my bike," Sara said. "In fact, he wants to be my rabbit so he can ride on my bike all the time."

"No! No!" Hairball leaped about frantically, but every time she got close to the bike, Sara nudged her away with the wheel.

After a few minutes of this, Sara got bored and tossed the rabbit up in the air. Hairball screamed as she watched the rabbit fly over her head and land in the branches of a tree in our front yard.

"Get him down!" Hairball clutched at Sara. "He's afraid up there, Sara, he's afraid."

"Nonsense." Sara shoved Hairball aside. "Rabbits love trees," she said and pedaled away, leaving Hairball sobbing at the foot of the tree.

Just as I stepped out on the front porch, Jamie came running around the side of the house. When he saw the rabbit stuck in the tree, he dashed up the steps and grabbed my hand. Pulling me toward the tree, he said, "Look, Emily, Mr. Bunny's in the tree. Can you get him down for Jennifer? Please, Emily?"

Looking up and down the street, I saw no sign of Sara, so I shrugged and walked over to the tree.

"Can you get him down, Emily, can you?" Jamie asked, patting Hairball's shaking shoulders.

"I guess so." I looked around for Sara again and then I jumped up, grabbed the lowest limb, and scrambled up into the tree. Thanks to Sara's strong throwing arm, Mr. Bunny was a good twelve feet off the ground and lodged firmly near the end of a long, thin limb. At first I tried standing on a limb near the trunk and shaking the branch holding the rabbit, but when Hairball saw Mr. Bunny flying up and down she started crying all over again.

"No, no, he's scared of falling. Please don't make Mr. Bunny fall, please, please," she sobbed.

Gritting my teeth, I wiggled out on the limb, hoping it wouldn't break. My only consolation was the thought that a broken bone might serve as an excuse to miss Ginny's party.

While Hairball and Jamie silently watched, I stretched out my hand and grabbed Mr. Bunny, jerking him a little to free him, and making the limb sway dangerously. With him safely in my hand, I inched my way back to the trunk and climbed slowly down, feeling a little weak in the knees and elbows. As I dropped to the grass, I heard Jamie say, "I knew Emily could get him."

Oh, thank you," Hairball cried as I handed her the rabbit. "Mr. Bunny, Mr. Bunny," she crooned, rocking him in her arms like a baby.

"Nothing to it," I lied, feeling kind of proud of myself.

The screech of bike tires brought my moment of glory to a sudden end. Taking one look at Sara, Hairball clasped Mr. Bunny to her chest and tore into our house, with Jamie right behind her.

"Did you get that stupid rabbit out of the tree?" Sara asked.

I shook my head. "It fell out of the tree all by itself, Sara. I just happened to be standing here, that's all."

Sara looked at me suspiciously. "Are you still being punished?"

I nodded.

"You shouldn't put up with that kind of stuff. I'd never let my parents get away with it."

"Emily Sherwood, come into this house!" Mother shouted from the front door.

Sara spun a pedal with her foot. "Well, I've been having a great time riding my bike and all. Too bad you haven't been able to come."

Watching her pedal away, I wondered what she'd do if she had parents like mine. Run away to California or something?

Later that afternoon, I was sitting in the kitchen snacking on cookies and milk. I could hear Hairball and Jamie talking on the back porch.

"When I grow up," Hairball was saying, "I'm going to buy a bulldozer and one day I'm going to be driving it down the road and Sara is going to be waiting to cross the road on her bike. I'm going to stop and say she can cross, and when she's right in front of me, do you know what I'm going to do?"

"Run over her!" Jamie shouted.

"Right! I'm going to run over her and smash her flat and all her bones will go crunch crunch crunch. And so will her bike. And I'll drive away laughing and she'll be flat on the road, so flat nobody can even pick her up."

"Vroom! Vroom! Vroom vroom vroom!" Jamie made a bulldozer sound and Hairball laughed.

"I hate Sara," she said. "I hate her, I hate her, I hate her! Do you hate Emily?"

Jamie hesitated. "Only sometimes, only when she's mean to me."

"Sara's mean all the time and I hate her all the time. And Mr. Bunny hates her too. Don't you, Mr. Bunny?"

Not waiting for Mr. Bunny's reply, Jamie asked, "Want to play in the sandbox?"

After they'd gone, I sat at the table for a while, thinking about what Hairball had said. I wondered if Sara had any idea that her little sister was plotting a horrible death for her. In a way it was funny. Who'd imagine such a skinny, helpless-looking kid could even think up such awful things?

TEN

I woke up on Saturday knowing that it was the day of the party. Mrs. Barnett hadn't called to disinvite me, as I'd hoped she might. I wasn't sick, I wasn't dying, and I didn't have enough money to run away. There wasn't anything to do but get up and hope that Sunday would come very quickly.

All day I moped around complaining of stomach aches, but the only person who gave me any sympathy was Jamie. He brought me a glass of Kool-Aid and drew me three pictures of rainbows to cheer me up. He even offered to read me *The Little Engine That Could*, but I thanked him and explained that I just wasn't in the right mood. He looked a little disappointed, but I think he understood.

A little after six o'clock, Mother helped me get dressed. She'd gone shopping with Maggy's mother earlier in the week and picked out an outfit that Mrs.

Rhodes said was perfect. The slacks were okay, but I hated the blouse. It had puffy sleeves and lacy trimming, and the material was printed all over with pastel flowers. It looked like the sort of thing Sandy would just love . . . but not on me.

As a finishing touch, Mother curled my hair and made me try a little makeup.

"There, Emily." She smiled at me in the mirror, and for the first time I realized that someday I would be as old as she was. "See how pretty you look when you fix yourself up?"

I looked away from our reflections, wishing my nose didn't have such a big bump at the end and wondering why I was at least two inches taller than my mother. I was afraid Mother wanted to have some embarrassing mother-daughter talk about parties and appearances and popularity and stuff like that. "I'd better go," I said.

She walked to the front door with me. "Have a good time," she said.

Daddy looked up from the television. "Just stay away from Sara Slater," he said. "And for heaven's sake, stand up straight."

"Do I look all right?"

"Of course. Behave yourself." He turned back to the news and I left the house.

Jamie was playing with a truck on the sidewalk. "You look pretty, Emily," he said.

"Thank you, Jamie." I bent down and gave him a hug. Then I started up the sidewalk toward Ginny's house. If Mother hadn't been watching me from the front door, I would have gone over to Sara's, but she didn't give me a chance.

Mrs. Barnett opened the door. "My, Emily, don't you look nice," she said in one of those phony voices adults reserve for children and senile old ladies. "The party is in the backyard."

On trembling legs, I followed her down the hall, through the kitchen, and out onto the back porch. Balloons and crepe paper streamers fluttered in the trees, a picnic table piled high with food stood in the center of the lawn, and groups of kids milled around on the grass. All the girls were on one side of the picnic table and the boys were on the other.

The first thing I noticed was that I would have to walk past Froggy, Jeff, and Tommy Lawson to get to the girls' side of the table. They were bunched together between the steps and the table, stuffing potato chips in their mouths and laughing at something, probably one of Froggy's dirty jokes. He must know a million of them, and everybody always laughs at them, no matter how dumb they are.

Some of the jerkier boys, like Calvin Kelly and David Porter, were playing soccer with a soda can. They were acting goofy and laughing it up, but they were staying as far away as possible from Froggy and his group. They knew better than to draw too much attention to themselves when Froggy was around.

The other boys were wandering around eating. Except Bruce. He was chasing Sandy and trying to drop a handful of ice down the back of her blouse. She was screaming and pretending to be mad, but it was obvious that she loved every minute of it.

Ginny and Maggy were giggling together and looking at Jeff, hoping he would start chasing them with ice cubes so they wouldn't have to hear Sandy brag about being the only girl any of the boys bothered. Unfortunately, Jeff was too busy laughing at Froggy's jokes to notice.

Next to Maggy and Ginny, Catherine Simpson, Julia Cisco, and Becky Ornstein were drinking Cokes and behaving like adults, as usual. Catherine and Julia are the quietest girls I know, the kind my mother calls thoughtful and mature and I call old before their time. Not to mention boring. Becky is the smartest girl in our class and also the dullest. And the most conceited.

Nowhere did I see Sara.

"Here's Emily," Mrs. Barnett said as if she were a page at the king's ball. Everybody stopped talking for a couple of seconds and stared at me.

Pretending not to notice that no one seemed ecstatic or even slightly pleased to see me, I walked slowly down the steps, staring hard at a tree a little to the left of the picnic table so I wouldn't have to look at anybody. I guess the news of my friendship with Sara had reached all my old friends and I was now a bigger outcast than Calvin Kelly.

As I walked past Froggy, I heard the word "giraffe," but I pretended not to. For a minute I had a sensation I often have, that none of this was really happening, that it wasn't my real life at all but a role I was playing in a movie. At any minute the director would say, "Cut," and we'd all start laughing and sit down and talk about the scene, and we'd all agree that it was really hard for a bunch of friends to pretend to hate each other.

Unfortunately, nobody said, "Cut," and I realized I had to find somebody to talk to. I couldn't just stand there on the edge of the crowd completely alone. In two minutes I'd burst into tears and totally disgrace myself. So, not knowing what else to do, I sidled up to Catherine Simpson, hoping to take advantage of her thoughtful maturity.

To my relief, Catherine seemed pleased to get involved in a polite conversation about what we'd been doing all summer. But the whole time she was describing the complicated macramé projects she'd made in the county recreation program, I kept looking up at the back porch and wondering where Sara was.

"I love your blouse," Catherine said, finally exhausting the subject of macramé.

"Thank you. I like yours too," I said, even though I didn't.

"Really? You don't think it makes me look fat or anything?"

Hoping that I wasn't blushing, I shook my head vigorously. "Oh, no, not at all," I said, proud of my own rapidly developing thoughtful maturity.

Just as I was about to fill up the slowly widening silence with one of my clever remarks about the weather, Mrs. Barnett announced Sara's arrival.

This time the silence was longer than it had been for me. And with good reason. I don't think anybody in College Hills had ever gone to a party with a guest like Sara. For one thing, she towered over Mrs. Barnett and everybody else, thanks to a pair of sandals with soles almost a foot thick. For another thing, every girl at the party was wearing some sort of ruffly blouse and a pair of slacks. Not Sara. She was wearing a long, sleeveless dress, cut low in front, mostly black but splashed with large pink and orange flowers. Her thick hair, still kinked from being braided, hung to her waist and bushed out around her face and body like a furry wrap. Big golden hoops dangled from her ears and her arms glittered with bracelets.

She looked at us with one eyebrow raised, a trick I'd been working on without success since our fight with Sandy. Everybody, including Mrs. Barnett, stared at her.

Finally Froggy broke the silence. "Who in the world is that?" he asked, his voice carrying across the lawn.

As if that was the cue she'd been waiting for, Sara slowly descended the steps, a little unsteadily on account of the sandals. Looking Froggy straight in the eye, she walked coolly across the lawn.

When she was one inch away from Froggy and about two feet above him, she leaned down, never breaking eye contact, and said, "Sara Adams Slater."

Before he could think of a single nasty crack, she stepped around him and approached the refreshment table. Sandy, Ginny, and Maggy bunched together and started giggling, and Catherine Simpson shifted slightly toward Julia and Becky, leaving me standing all by myself.

"Am I glad to see you," I said to Sara. "I was beginning to think you weren't coming."

"What? Miss this glorious party? Me?" Scooping up a handful of potato chips, Sara stuffed at least a dozen into her mouth.

"Are you wearing makeup?" I stared at her eyes. They were outlined heavily in black and the lids glistened with a green coating. Her cheeks were smeared with bright pink blusher, her lips were scarlet, and so were her nails, both finger and toe.

"Of course. I thought since I had to come to this

great party, I might as well give everybody something to talk about. Right?''

''Where did you get that dress?''

''Oh, Mom made it last night in a fit of creativity. Isn't it great? Believe it or not, it's a designer pattern.''

''Well, it's different,'' I said, trying to figure out what game Sara was playing.

''You don't have to lie, Em,'' Sara said in a more natural voice. ''I know it's hideous, but it's what my mother thinks kids wear to parties. Maybe in New York they do.'' Sara struck a zany pose, the kind models twist themselves into for fashion magazines, and we cracked up.

''Come on,'' Sara said, ''I think Mrs. Barnett is getting ready to serve the food.''

We found two chairs near the picnic table, and Mrs. Barnett handed us each a paper plate piled high with potato salad, more potato chips, and two hot dogs.

Sara poked at the pale mound of potato salad suspiciously. ''I never eat anything with mayonnaise on it at a picnic,'' she said. ''It spoils fast and you can get ptomaine poisoning and die a horrible death.''

Shoving the potato salad aside, she picked up her hot dog and bit into it. ''Ugh.'' She made a face and put it down. ''This hot dog's not pure beef,'' she said loudly. ''It's the cheap kind, full of chemicals and dangerous additives. I'm not eating these.''

Several kids stared at her and poked at their own

food, but most of them ate it anyway. Thinking it was kind of strange for Sara to be this particular about what she ate, I sat next to her holding my soggy plate, the food on it untouched. I hadn't eaten much all day and I was hungry, but I certainly couldn't touch tainted food. Not with Sara sitting right there next to me.

After everyone else had finished, Mrs. Barnett brought out a huge birthday cake. On top was a cheerleader made of pink icing and surrounded by twelve candles. Mrs. Barnett hadn't told any of us it was Ginny's birthday. Ginny blushed and said she didn't want us to, but Mrs. Barnett made us all sing "Happy Birthday." Sara nudged me, and I started laughing because Froggy was singing off key, but somehow we got through it and Ginny blew out her candles.

Sara nudged me again. "Did you ever think how many germs and drops of saliva get all over a cake when people blow candles out?"

I shook my head. Why did Sara have to tell me that? Here I was, with a plate of food on the grass by my feet, starving, thinking how great a piece of cake was going to taste, and she had to go and ruin it all.

As Ginny started cutting the cake, Mrs. Barnett stood on the back porch smiling, and Mr. Barnett crept around the yard snapping pictures with a little Instamatic camera. I couldn't help noticing that he never once aimed the camera at Sara and me.

Then Froggy leaned forward and asked Ginny in a low voice, "Which part of the cheerleader do I get?"

Ginny pretended not to hear him, but all the boys started laughing, even Calvin Kelly, who couldn't possibly have heard what Froggy said.

"I want her sweater," Tommy sputtered, choking with laughter.

"I'll take her leg," Jeff snickered.

"And I'll take . . ." Froggy lowered his voice and whispered something to Bruce that made him crack up.

With a red face, Ginny passed the cake around, trying to ignore the boys. I glanced over at Mrs. Barnett. She and Mr. Barnett were still standing on the back porch smiling at everybody and thinking what a nice party it was.

When Ginny handed me my cake and ice cream, I was almost glad I'd come, but just as I opened my mouth to taste it, I heard Sara say, "No, thank you. I never eat cake somebody blew all over."

For a minute I thought that Ginny was going to shove the plate in Sara's face, but somehow she managed to restrain herself. Shrugging, she handed the cake to Becky, who took it without a murmur.

I sat there staring at the cake, devil's food, my favorite kind. The ice cream was just starting to melt, the way I like it best. I looked at Sara. She looked at me, one eyebrow raised. I knew she wanted me to return mine, but I couldn't. It was too much of a sacrifice. I lowered my eyes and silently ate my cake, germs or no germs. After all, Ginny looked perfectly healthy.

ELEVEN

After we finished eating, Ginny led us down to the recreation room. She and Maggy turned on the record player and said it was time to dance, but the boys didn't seem interested in dancing. Following Froggy's lead, most of them herded together on the other side of the room around a washtub full of ice and Cokes.

Looking at the other girls standing around stiffly waiting for boys to ask them to dance, Sara said, "Let's get a Coke."

"But the boys," I said.

"What about them?"

"That's where they are," I whispered.

"So? They don't own the Cokes, do they?" Sara started across the room and I followed her.

"Excuse me," she said, pushing herself between Froggy and Jeff. "Here, Emily." She handed me a dripping bottle. "Where's the opener?" she asked Froggy.

"Wouldn't you like to know?" Froggy said.

"Here it is." Jeff held it up, but as Sara reached for it he tossed it to Bruce. Around and around the bottle opener went with Sara desperately grabbing at it, her hair flying.

At last Tommy Lawson dropped it, but, as Sara dove for it, Froggy put his foot on it.

"You aren't really thirsty, are you? Cokes are bad for you anyway. They're full of chemicals and dangerous additives, and besides, they rot your teeth and put hair on your chest." Froggy laughed so loudly that Sandy came scurrying across the room, eager not to miss anything.

"Hey," Froggy said, "What do you all think a nice little girl should say to get the opener?"

Sara looked at him coldly. "Since I'm not a nice little girl, how would I know?" she said, and walked away with me so close behind her I was practically stepping on her heels.

"Hey, Emily," Froggy called, "do you sit up and beg too?"

I looked at him blankly.

"Well, you seem like such a nice little puppy dog, heeling like that and all."

"Just watch out she doesn't bite you," Sara snarled.

"Oh, I'm so scared, I'm really scared." Froggy

backed away, his eyes rolling. "Please don't sic Emily on me, Sara, please don't!"

Everybody looked at us and laughed.

"Here, Emily, here, Emily, Emily, Emily, good girl, come on now," Tommy Lawson spluttered, flashing his braces and spraying saliva all over the place.

"Let's leave," I whispered to Sara. I wanted to go home before I started crying.

"Leave? The party's just starting to get interesting," Sara said.

"Hey," Maggy shouted, "isn't anybody going to dance? We've got lots of good records."

"Yeah, let's do the dog-trot," Froggy shouted. "That's Emily's favorite dance. She's real good at it."

"Come on," Maggy said. "Let's dance."

"Would you rather play Pass the Orange?" Ginny asked; holding up an orange. "Does everybody know how?"

Several people, including me, didn't, so Ginny and Maggy demonstrated how you passed the orange from person to person without touching it with your hands. You had to get awfully close to the person next to you and get it out from under his chin with your chin. I didn't want to play, but Ginny divided us into two teams, lining us up boy, girl, boy, girl.

I was on Maggy's team, sort of in the middle, behind Tommy and in front of Calvin, and Sara was on Ginny's team, near the end of the line. She was supposed to pass her orange to Froggy, which was Ginny's idea of a joke, I guess.

"I'm not playing," Sara said and sat down on the couch, her arms folded across her chest, her face expressionless.

"But you have to!" Ginny said.

"No, I don't. I don't have to do anything I don't feel like doing."

"Let her sit there," Froggy said. "Who wants her for a partner anyway? I'll get at the end of the other line and then I'll have Catherine for a partner." He sidled over to Catherine and tried to put his arm around her, but she wiggled away, giving Sara a dirty look.

"No," Maggy said. "That's not fair. We'll have more people on our team."

"Well, how about if I stand up here in front of Ginny, then?" Froggy said, giving her what he thought was a very sexy smile.

"But I'm the captain!" Ginny said.

"How long does it take you to catch on, Froggy?" Sara said, leaning back on the couch and examining the polish on her fingernails.

"Huh?" Froggy popped his eyes at Sara.

"Don't you know why nobody wants to be your partner?"

"What are you talking about?"

Maggy and Ginny exchanged worried looks, but everybody else was staring at Sara.

"You're absolutely disgusting, don't you know that? Your eyes pop out. Boing! Boing!" Sara opened her eyes wide and popped them at Froggy. "And you're some kind of a sex maniac, too. Just ask Sandy, she'll tell you."

As Froggy started across the room toward Sara, she grabbed a pillow and jumped up on the couch. Standing there brandishing the pillow like a weapon, she looked around the room. "What are you laughing at, Tommy Tinmouth?" she shouted. "Don't you know that you're giving everybody within ten feet of you a shower?" She held her pillow in front of her. "Don't get me wet—I took a bath before I left home."

"Shut up, Skyscraper!" Sandy screamed.

"Just ignore her!" Ginny turned the record player up louder, trying to drown out Sara.

But Sara kept on yelling the things we'd overheard at Maggy's window. "Has Bruce asked you to go with him yet, Sandy? Huh? Has he?"

Sandy lunged at Sara, but she danced away from her down the couch.

"I told my mother not to invite her!" Ginny cried. "I knew she'd ruin everything!"

"Oh, Ginny, have I got some news for you," Sara said. "Ask Froggy and Jeff what they write on walls about you. I can't tell you what it is—I'm not that crude—but I sure hope it isn't true." And Sara threw the pillow at Froggy as hard as she could, hitting him right in the face with it.

"You crazy creep!" Froggy charged at Sara and tackled her. They fell backwards across the couch, taking the only lamp with them. When it crashed to the floor, the room went black.

The next few minutes were like one of those crazy Laurel and Hardy movie scenes. You know, the kind where Laurel throws a pie at Hardy and Hardy ducks and the pie hits someone else who then grabs another pie and hits someone else until about a hundred people are covered with meringue and shouting and screaming and carrying on like maniacs.

Suddenly the overhead light flashed on, and there was Mr. Barnett. For a second everybody froze. Froggy and Sara were sprawled on the couch, which was now halfway across the room, its pillows strewn everywhere. The rest of us were scattered around the room like a bunch of kids playing statues.

The first person to make a sound was Calvin. He started giggling.

"Oh, Daddy," Ginny wailed. "It was all Sara's fault, she started the whole thing!" Bursting into tears, Ginny pushed past her father and ran up the stairs.

By this time, Froggy had moved away from Sara and was tucking his shirt in. Sara stood alone in the middle of the room. A Coke had spilled at her feet.

Her dress was wrinkled, her mascara had run and formed dark circles under her eyes, and her hair stood out in a frizzy cloud around her face. With her arms folded across her chest, she stared at Mr. Barnett, a smirky smile on her face.

"Well, do you have anything to say for yourself?" Mr. Barnett thundered.

Sara shrugged and continued to smirk.

"And you?" He turned to Froggy.

"Me? What did I do?" Froggy's voice cracked indignantly.

"I think you both should leave so the other children can enjoy themselves," Mr. Barnett said.

"Why me? I told you I didn't do anything," Froggy said. "She started it, not me. Anybody here can tell you that."

"He's right," Sandy said, smiling up at Mr. Barnett. "It wasn't Froggy's fault. He shouldn't have to leave."

Mr. Barnett looked around for Mrs. Barnett to tell him what to do, but she must have been upstairs with Ginny. In confusion, he turned back to Sandy.

"Just send her home. With her gone, everything will be fine," Sandy said, smiling.

Everybody nodded.

"Well," Mr. Barnett said uneasily, frowning at Sara, "what do you have to say?"

"Only that this is the most boring party I've ever

been to and I'll be glad to go home. Who wants to associate with morons anyway?'' Without looking at me or anybody else, Sara started walking calmly toward the stairs.

Standing there in my safe little corner, I realized that nobody had said a word about me. I could stay at the party as long as I wanted to. I didn't have to leave in disgrace and face a terrible scene with my parents. Nervously I looked around the room, trying to decide what to do.

Catherine and Julia were whispering together as they watched Sara start up the steps. They looked shocked, and when they glanced at me, their eyes were cool.

Then my eyes met Maggy's, but she quickly turned away, her eyes seeking Sandy's, and I was sure she didn't care whether I stayed or left.

Meanwhile, Sara was halfway up the steps, her crazy dress dragging behind her. I wanted to cross the room and follow her outside, but I was scared to walk past Mr. Barnett. Furthermore, I was pretty sure that Froggy would make some kind of crack and everybody would laugh at me. For a moment, I considered locking myself in the bathroom until the party was over and then sneaking home. But I wasn't sure what I'd do if someone wanted to use it.

When Sara was almost to the top of the stairs, I made up my mind. Sara was my friend and if she left

I had to go with her. There really wasn't any choice. Feeling my heartbeat soar, I stepped out of my corner, crossed the room, and put my foot on the bottom step.

"Where do you think you're going, Emily?" Mr. Barnett asked.

"With Sara," I whispered.

"Bow wow wow," Froggy barked.

TWELVE

At the end of Ginny's sidewalk, I caught up with Sara. "What are we going to do now?" I asked. "It's only nine o'clock and the party's supposed to last till ten-thirty."

Sara shrugged and sat down on the curb. "First I'm going to take these dumb shoes off," she said, bending down and unbuckling them. She stretched her feet and wiggled her toes. "How do you like my toenails? Midnight Scarlet Secret."

"It looks like black blood or something."

"That's what I thought." She yawned.

"What do you want to do?" I asked, hoping she'd come up with something good.

"I don't know. Let's just walk around for a while," Sara said.

With her sandals dangling from one hand, Sara started up the street and I followed her. A chorus of insects chirped in the trees around us, their voices rising, falling, stopping, and then starting all over again, like people talking at a party.

"What are we going to tell our parents?" I asked, wishing I could make the locusts shut up.

"I'll think of something, don't worry," Sara said, swinging her sandals.

I looked at her, puzzled. She didn't seem like herself at all. I'd expected her to have a great plan for the rest of the night, but here she was, just moping along, hardly saying a word. If I hadn't known her better, I'd have thought she was just as worried as I was.

"Are you mad at me or something?" I asked her after we'd walked a couple of blocks without saying anything.

"Why should I be mad at you?"

"I don't know," I said. Whenever people stop talking to me, I assume they're mad at me. If the silent person is my mother, I'm usually right.

"Don't you ever wonder how people stand it?" Sara asked suddenly.

"Stand what?"

"This, all of it." She waved her sandals at the tidy little houses crouching in their own shadows on either side of the street. "Don't they get bored? Don't they feel trapped?"

I shrugged. "Probably they never even think about it."

"But do you think life has to be like this?"

"No, you could be a movie star or a rock singer and travel all over the world in your own private jet." I could just see Sara getting off a plane in Hollywood or somewhere, wearing her long dress and scarlet nail polish, sneering at everybody the way she did at the party.

"People like Sandy and those other jerks, they'll never go anywhere or do anything," Sara said. "They'll just get married and have kids and spend all their lives trapped in little houses like these. I'd hate to be like Sandy, wouldn't you?"

I nodded, but I wasn't so sure I was telling the truth. I couldn't see myself getting off a private jet in Hollywood. And if you're doomed to live a boring, mediocre life, you might as well be pretty and popular.

As if she knew what I was thinking, Sara said, "Maybe you could be my agent, Em, and we could travel everywhere together. Wouldn't that be great?" Piling her hair up on top of her head, Sara sighed. "I'm so hot everything is sticking to me. I feel like I'm wearing a fur coat."

"Want to go home?"

"Might as well." Sara turned around and started back down the street. Suddenly she stopped, threw her head back, and gave the most blood-curdling scream I'd ever heard. Still screaming, she started running down the street and I followed her, adding a few screams of my own just in case she had seen something I hadn't seen.

Behind us, I heard voices and, on both sides of the street, porch lights flashed on. Turning a corner, Sara raced across a lawn, jumped a hedge, cut across an empty lot, and finally stopped, gasping for breath, on our corner. In the distance we could hear dogs barking frantically.

"What was that for? Why did you scream?" I panted.

"Just to see if anyone was alive," Sara said. "Come on, race you home!"

Holding a sandal in each hand, she tore down the street, her hair flying, and I ran after her, straining every muscle to beat her.

Thinking I might be ahead, I flew up my front steps and, as I opened the door, turned my head to see where Sara was. What a mistake! The next thing I knew, I was flat on my back with a horrible pain in my head and blood everywhere.

"Emily!" Mother screamed, running toward me with Daddy close behind her. "What happened?"

Somehow I made them understand that my head and the edge of the front door had collided. After they got over their hysteria, they stopped the bleeding and led me upstairs to bed. The last thing I remember thinking was that they'd never had a chance to ask me why I'd gotten home so early from Ginny's party.

*   *   *

The next morning I was lying in bed wondering if Mother would expect me to get up and come downstairs for breakfast. Hearing someone coming up the steps, I closed my eyes and pretended to be asleep, hoping Mother was bringing me breakfast in bed. For good measure, I moaned a little, thinking that the sorrier she felt for me the less likely she was to ask me questions about the party.

"Emily?"

It was Sara. I sat up, feeling a little weak.

"How's your head?" She sat down at the foot of my bed. "You look terrible."

"Thanks," I said. "I feel terrible too."

"Did you say anything about the party?"

I shook my head, wincing at the little throbs the sudden movement caused. "I was too busy bleeding."

"That's great. It gives us a chance to make our stories match. Listen, here's what I told my parents." She paused and looked around to make sure Mother hadn't sneaked up the stairs and hidden behind the door.

"Okay, we were at the party, right?" She leaned forward, her voice tense and low. "When we went down to the recreation room, Ginny turned out the light so we could play kissing games, but you and I didn't want to. So everybody made fun of us and called us goody-goodies. When the game started,

105

Froggy was supposed to be my partner. He grabbed me and started kissing me and I was fighting him off. He had me on the couch and was trying to reach down the front of my dress. As I struggled to get away, I kicked the lamp over.''

Sara made it sound so real, I almost believed it had really happened that way.

"Then the light went on and Mr. Barnett saw Froggy and me on the couch," Sara continued. "Everybody else had heard Mr. Barnett coming and gotten themselves together, so he didn't know what was actually going on. Besides, they all made up a bunch of lies so he wouldn't figure it out. Okay?''

I nodded. "But what was I doing?"

"Trying to hide from Calvin Kelly.''

"That's what I'm supposed to tell Mother?"

"You'd better, or you'll get me in a lot of trouble, Em," Sara said grimly.

"But I don't tell lies very well, Sara. Nobody ever believes me.''

"You'd better start practicing, then." She got up and began looking at my china horse collection. "Are you going to stay in bed all day?"

Although I would have liked to say yes, I sat up and put my feet on the floor. My head throbbed and the room spun a little.

"Look at your blouse, it's got blood all over it." Sara picked it up from the floor and held it aloft by

106

one sleeve. "It looks like evidence for a murder trial. We should stuff it in a storm sewer and see what happens. I bet the police would be combing College Hills for a body."

Snatching the blouse out of Sara's hand, I tossed it into my dirty clothes basket. For some reason, the thought of being a bloody corpse didn't amuse me.

"I was only kidding, Em. Come on, where's your sense of humor?" Sara ambled out the door. "I'll wait for you downstairs. And be sure you have the story straight, okay?"

As Sara thumped down the steps, I staggered around, putting on shorts and looking for a shirt that buttoned down the front. I was afraid to pull a T-shirt over my head. I might start bleeding again.

Downstairs, Sara was sitting at the kitchen table, drinking a cup of coffee and telling Mother about the party.

"It was just awful," she was saying. "The jokes they were making and all. I didn't know kids around here acted like that. Mom is sorry we left New York."

"Sara, are you sure you're not exaggerating?" Mother asked.

Sara shook her head, her eyes wide. "Honest, Mrs. Sherwood, it was terrible. Wasn't it, Emily?"

I nodded. "It was the worst party I've ever been to, Mother." I looked her right in the eye because that was certainly the truth.

"Well, I don't know what to say," Mother said. "If I'd only known what the party was going to be like, I'd have never made you go, Emily. I thought they were such sweet girls." She stirred her coffee. "I'm proud of you two, though, for being strong enough to say no. After all, it isn't easy to refuse to participate in something everyone else wants to do." She put her arms around me and gave me a hug.

Embarrassed, I pulled away and put two slices of bread in the toaster. I wondered if Sara felt as bad as I did listening to Mother praise our high moral standards. When I glanced at her over Mother's shoulder, though, she winked and gave me a victory sign.

THIRTEEN

A couple of afternoons later, Sara and I were sitting under a tree in her front yard. It was so hot I could hardly breathe. Even the leaves on the trees looked hot. They hung in the still air, limp and dusty, swaying slightly. Like Sara and me, they were waiting for something to happen. A cool breeze. A rainstorm. Autumn.

The screen door slammed, and Hairball came out. She sat down on the front step and stuck her thumb in her mouth. As usual, she had Mr. Bunny with her.

"Look at her." Sara scowled at Hairball. "Six years old and still sucking her thumb. What a disgusting kid."

"She's not so bad," I said, remembering how sorry I'd felt for Hairball last week.

"I've got a great idea," Sara said, ignoring me. "Just go along with whatever I say, okay?"

She got up and walked across the lawn. When Hairball saw her coming, she snatched her thumb out of her mouth like it was poison and hugged Mr. Bunny. She looked a little uneasy when Sara sat down next to her and put her arm around her. She wasn't used to affection from Sara.

"Oh, Hairball," Sara sighed, "I hardly know how to tell you this or how I'm going to get through my part of it. We'll both just have to be brave, Hairball, very very brave."

"What are you talking about, Sara? Why do we have to be brave?" Hairball's chin wobbled, and from where I stood I could see a tear in her eye.

"How can I tell you?" Sara moaned. "Oh, it's just so awful!"

"What? What?" Hairball was standing up now, her eyes enormous.

"Oh, alas, alas, poor little Hairball!" Sara lowered her voice to a whisper and looked fearfully around the yard as if someone were lurking in the bushes. Nervously I glanced behind me, but I didn't see anything.

"Today's the day, Hairball," Sara went on, "the day we've been dreading all these years."

"You mean the gypsy woman's here? She's come to get me?" Hairball looked desperate. She hugged Mr. Bunny tightly, her face white.

"Yes." Sara embraced Hairball. "Yes, little Hairball, and I'm the one she's chosen to bring you to her.

Along with Emily. She has to help me.'' Sara shot me a look that plainly said I'd better stop standing around on one foot like a lovesick whooping crane and get busy.

"Oh, no, Sara! No, no, you wouldn't, Sara, you wouldn't!'' Hairball screamed, tears spurting out of her eyes.

But Sara dragged Hairball across the lawn, ignoring her screams, and motioned me to help. Half-heartedly I grabbed Hairball's feet, and the two of us carted her down the street. I kept thinking I should say something, but I knew how much Sara hated criticism. I was afraid that if I told her to leave Hairball alone, she'd get mad at me, so I just followed Sara's lead, struggling to keep my hold on Hairball's ankles. For a scrawny little kid, she was pretty strong.

When we got to the railroad tracks, Sara stopped and told me to let go of Hairball's feet. Never loosening her grip on Hairball's arms, Sara looked around. Above Hairball's shrieks, I could hear a train whistle blowing for the Riverside crossing about two miles away.

"Come on, Hairball.'' Sara jerked her toward the bunker.

"Let me go, Sara, let me go!'' Hairball cried.

"This is where you have to wait for the old gypsy,'' Sara said, pulling Hairball onto the roof of the bunker.

"No, Sara, no! Not the bunker! No, not down there! No, no!" Hairball twisted and turned like a demented monkey, but she wasn't strong enough to pull away from Sara.

"Come on, Sara," I said feebly. "Why don't we go up to the shopping center and get a Coke or something?"

"Open the trap door, Em!" Sara shouted, holding Hairball with both hands.

"You're not really going to put her down there, are you?" I asked.

"Of course! That's where the old gypsy woman wants her," Sara screamed at me. "Hold still!" she snarled at poor frantic Hairball.

"Sara," I said, my mouth dry. Why was it so hard to say what I really thought? Was Froggy right about me? Maybe I really was a whimpering puppy dog. "You're kidding, aren't you?" I shouted to make myself heard over Hairball's screams and the whistle of the approaching train.

"Open it, Emily!" Sara yelled. Her face was red and beads of sweat stood out on her upper lip.

"Sara, you know, I don't think we . . . I mean, it's not really . . ."

"Are you going to help me or not?" Sara screamed. The train was blowing its whistle again, louder and nearer, and I could feel the bunker's tin roof starting to vibrate under my bare feet.

Just then Hairball lost her grip on Mr. Bunny and he flew out of her arms. I saw him land several feet away on the railroad tracks.

"Sara, couldn't we just—" I started.

But Sara didn't let me finish. Calling me one of the names she usually reserved for Sandy, she let go of one of Hairball's arms and tried to lift the door by herself.

"Leave her alone! Leave her alone!" I shouted. Grabbing Hairball's free arm, I tried to pull her away from Sara.

Suddenly Hairball pulled away from both of us. Before either one of us could stop her, she leaped off the bunker and started running toward the train tracks.

"Come back here!" Sara shouted, but the train was a lot closer and its whistle was blowing for the College Hills crossing.

Without thinking, I jumped after Hairball and ran toward her. "Hairball! The train, the train!" I shouted.

She didn't pay any attention to me. All she was thinking about was that dumb rabbit lying on the tracks. Behind me, I could hear Sara shrieking something, but I didn't turn around.

"Hairball! Hairball!" I shouted, but she didn't stop. And all the time the train was getting bigger and bigger and nearer and nearer and the air was full of its whistle and rattle and roar.

As Hairball bent down to grab the rabbit, I lunged

forward and shoved her off the tracks. The train roared past, screeching and hissing, its whistle screaming at us. Scared to move, I clutched Hairball and watched car after car bounce past us. Boxcars, gondolas, tankers, piggybacks stacked with new cars, there must have been a hundred of them, but I wasn't capable of counting them at that point.

Finally the caboose rattled past, and I saw a man leaning out of a window shouting and shaking his fist instead of smiling and waving. I sat up, feeling like most of my bones had dissolved, and looked at Hairball. She was still huddled in a little ball, weeping. That's when I noticed she didn't have Mr. Bunny. She must have dropped him when I pushed her off the tracks. All that was left of him now were a few purple scraps scattered over the cinders.

On the other side of the tracks, I saw Sara kneeling on the roof of the bunker. Her face was hidden in her hands and her shoulders were shaking with sobs. Did she think Hairball and I had been killed by the train? Wanting to make her suffer, I was tempted to take Hairball and hide in the bushes farther up the bank.

As I watched, though, Sara spread her fingers apart and peeked through them the way people do during scary scenes in movies. I guess she was afraid she was going to see the bloody remains of Hairball and me strewn all over the place.

"Oh, God, I thought you were dead!" Sara cried when she saw us. Wiping her eyes with the back of her hand, she jumped off the bunker and ran across the tracks to us. "Are you all right?" she asked, her eyes still brimming with tears.

I nodded. Except for a few cuts and bruises, we were fine. A little shaky, but otherwise okay.

Hairball didn't say a word. She didn't even look at Sara. She just stood there sobbing. Her jugular vein stood out, a throbbing blue cord against her white skin, and her face was black with soot, except for two white streaks where her tears had washed the dirt away.

"Mr. Bunny, Mr. Bunny," Hairball wept, "he's all dead and gone."

Sara looked at her uncomfortably. Her face was so pale that her freckles stood out like brown spatter paint. "You can always get another one," she said sort of stiffly.

"There's not another Mr. Bunny in the whole world. I'll never see him again. Never, never, never."

"Well, you shouldn't have dragged him everywhere you go. It's a wonder you didn't lose him a long time ago," Sara muttered.

Hairball threw herself down on the cinders and cried harder. "You don't care! You don't care! You probably wish I was dead, too!"

Very slowly Sara reached out and touched Hairball's back. "That's not true, Hairball."

But Hairball pulled away from Sara's hand. "It is so! You've always hated me, ever since I was born you've hated me and hated me and hated me!"

Sara shook her head. "Come on, Hairball, I'll prove I don't hate you. I'll buy you a new rabbit, a really beautiful rabbit, the best rabbit in the whole world."

Hairball shuddered all over, trying to stop crying. "It wouldn't be Mr. Bunny, it wouldn't be him back again," she gasped.

"It'll be even better. It'll be all new and fuzzy." Sara patted Hairball again, and this time Hairball didn't pull away. "Really, Hairball, it'll be a beautiful rabbit."

Hairball sat up. She picked up a little scrap of Mr. Bunny and fondled it sadly. For a while she didn't say a word. Finally she looked at Sara.

"Will you get a purple rabbit?" she asked.

Sara nodded. "As purple as they come."

"Will it be as big as me?"

Sara nodded again. "I'll get the biggest one I can find."

While Hairball thought that over, Sara added, "And all you have to do to get the rabbit is promise not to tell Mom and Dad about what happened. Okay?"

Hairball looked up at Sara, her eyes narrowed. "You mean about the bunker and the train?"

"I'll get you anything, Hairball, anything at all, if you just promise not to tell."

"Will you promise to save me from the old gypsy woman? Can you make her go away forever?"

"You don't have to worry about her anymore, Hairball," Sara said. "Just as you jumped down on the train tracks, she drove up in her car. She thinks the train killed you. She'll never come back. I promise you."

"How about Rick-the-Rat-faced-Boy?"

"He was in the car with her. Neither one of them will come back. I heard them say so as they drove away."

"Do you promise?"

"I promise, Hairball. Even if they did come back, I'd chase them away and protect you. That's what big sisters are for, isn't it?"

"I don't know," Hairball said thoughtfully, wiping her nose on her sleeve.

"Well, what do you say?" Sara tried to smile in a sisterly way. "Is it a deal, Hairball?"

"Well, there *is* something else." Hairball looked at the grass growing on the sides of the railroad banks. Reaching out and pulling up a handful, she said softly, "I don't want you to call me that anymore. My name is Jennifer, and that's what I want you to call me. Nothing else. Just Jennifer."

Sara stared at Hairball as if she couldn't quite believe her ears. She hesitated a minute, then cleared her throat. "Okay." She nodded. "Sure, that's no big deal. I mean, it was just a nickname, but if you don't like it, it's all right with me."

"It's an awful name to call someone and I hate it," Hairball said.

Sara shrugged. "Well, I didn't make it up. It's what the old gypsy woman always called you. Remember, Em, when she drove up in the car last night to tell us her plans? Didn't she clearly say 'Hairball'?"

As Sara dug her elbow in my side, I looked at Hairball—the former Hairball, I should say. Her bony little shoulders were still shaking and her face looked absolutely pathetic all streaked with tears and soot.

"It's not true and you know it, Sara!" I shouted so loud she jumped and Hairball looked stunned. "It's not true! There wasn't any gypsy last night and there wasn't one today, not just now and not ever. You made it all up, Sara Slater! Stop lying to her!"

I had a glimpse of Hairball's frightened face as Sara slapped me. Then I slapped her back as hard as I could, and for the next few minutes we screamed insults at each other and grappled together, hitting and kicking, pulling hair and clawing. All of a sudden, the cut on my head broke open and blood started trickling down my face.

"Now look what you've done!" I screamed, pulling away from Sara.

"I hope you bleed to death!" she yelled.

Leaving her and Hairball on the railroad tracks, I ran for home, terrified at the sight of my own blood.

FOURTEEN

When Mother saw me running up the front steps with blood all over my face, she put me in the car and took me to the doctor.

"I knew you needed stitches," she said as we drove home afterward. "I told your father you'd do something to start it bleeding again."

I didn't answer. I just sat there, staring out the car window, feeling kind of drained. Having a circle of hair the size of a quarter shaved off my head and getting eight stitches, a tetanus shot, and a lecture on the care of scalp wounds hadn't left me in a very talkative mood. Particularly depressing was the fact that school started in four days. I would have to walk into Hyattstown Junior High School with a bald spot above my right temple.

"Does it hurt?" Jamie asked, leaning over the seat

to get a good look at the hideous black threads sticking out of my scalp.

I nodded, feeling sort of nauseated.

"Poor Emily." He offered me a bite of his Popsicle.

Why couldn't everybody be as nice to me as Jamie was?

For the next couple of days, I lay around the house complaining about my stitches and feeling sorry for myself. Although I was sure that Sara would appear any minute to apologize, she didn't come near our house. I thought about calling her, but every time I started to dial her number, I remembered how hard she'd slapped me and I got mad at her all over again. It seemed to me that she should call me. After all, she was the one who started the fight. Not me. And besides, for all she knew I could have developed blood poisoning or gangrene or something.

One afternoon while I was staring out the living room window, I saw Sara pedal by on her bike. Jennifer was riding on the back clutching a brand-new rabbit, twice as big and twice as purple as Mr. Bunny. Although Jennifer looked as if she were having the time of her life, Sara seemed glummer than ever. She didn't even glance at our house.

But Jennifer did. When she saw me standing at the window, she waved happily and held up the rabbit.

I waved back and sat down on the couch, trying to

interest myself in a soap opera Mother was watching. But I didn't know who all the people were or what they were talking about.

"Emily, what's the matter?" Mother looked up from the needlework design she was stitching. The only way she can justify watching television in the middle of the day is to do something useful at the same time.

I looked at the little owl she was working on. He had big, sad yellow eyes and I was glad she was going to hang him in Jamie's room. It would have made me uncomfortable to have those eyes staring at me all the time. I shook my head. "Nothing," I said.

"Have you and Sara quarreled?"

"You hate her anyway, so why should you care? You're probably glad!"

"Emily, I don't hate Sara," Mother said slowly. "It took me a while to get used to her, that's all. Her behavior at Ginny's party forced me to change my opinion of her. She's far more sensible than I originally thought."

I winced and looked at a man on the television screen trying to convince his wife that he still loved her even though there was another woman in his life. If I told Mother the truth about the party, she'd be furious. She'd never let me associate with Sara again. That is, if I ever wanted to.

"I hate to see you so unhappy, Emily," Mother said.

Before I had time to think about what I was doing, I threw my arms around Mother and started crying.

"Oh, Emily, now, now, don't cry, please don't cry." She sounded embarrassed and her body felt a little stiff, but she put her arms around me and let me sob on her shoulder.

"What's the matter with Emily?" I heard Jamie ask. "Is her head hurting again?"

"She's just feeling sad," Mother said.

I felt Jamie pat my arm. "Poor Emily," he said.

All of a sudden I started laughing. It seemed so funny being comforted by my five-year-old brother.

"Do you feel better?" Mother asked, just as the man on the television screen was replaced by a parade of cupcakes singing about how delicious they were.

I nodded, sort of sobbing and snorting at the same time.

"Let's all have Kool-Aid," Jamie said, and Mother and I followed him out to the kitchen.

After I drink mine, I went out in the backyard and sat down on the swing set. A few minutes later, I heard the Rhodeses' back door slam. Looking up, I saw Maggy standing on her steps staring at me. It was the first time I'd seen her since Ginny's party, so I wasn't sure whether to wave or to pretend I didn't see her. While I was hesitating, she came down her steps, crossed the yard, and walked up to the swing set.

"Mind if I sit down?" she asked.

I shook my head and she dropped onto the swing next to me. "Remember how high we used to think we could swing in these?" she asked.

I nodded.

"They seem so little now, I can hardly squeeze myself into the seat. If we pumped hard, we'd tip the whole dumb swing set over."

"I know."

"How's your head?" Maggy asked after a couple of seconds of silence. "Mom said you cut it after the party."

"It's better." I bent my head so she could see the stitches.

"Oh, Emily, that's horrible! School starts the day after tomorrow. What are you going to do?"

"I don't know. Maybe I've found a true advantage to being tall. Most people won't be able to see it, right?" To my surprise, I started to laugh. It was the first real joke I'd ever made about my height—not exactly the sort of comic routine that would get me on TV, but at least it was a start.

Maggy laughed, too. "That's one way to look at it!"

"If only I could figure out some way to stand up all day. As soon as I sit down, everybody will see it."

"You could wear a hat," Maggy said. "Or a wig."

"A blond one, with lots of curls. Or a red one. Or maybe I could shave my whole head and start a new fad."

"How come you left Ginny's party?" Maggy asked, suddenly changing the subject. "You didn't have to. Nobody was mad at you or anything."

I shrugged. "I just didn't want to stay there."

"Was it because of Froggy and all that dumb stuff he was saying? You know how he is. He talks like that all the time, it doesn't mean anything. You shouldn't take it seriously, Emily."

"I know."

"If you keep on hanging around with Sara, you'll never be popular. You know?" Maggy leaned forward confidentially. "Sara's weird, Emily. I mean it. How can you stand her?"

"When you get to know her she's not weird," I said. "You'd probably like her if you knew her better. You and Sara and I could have a lot of fun, Maggy."

"You've got to be kidding! I'd never hang around with a creep like Sara Slater."

Just then Sandy appeared in Maggy's backyard. "What are you doing over there, Mag?" she asked. "We're supposed to be up at Ginny's practicing cheer-leading. Barb's waiting for us."

"Want to come, Emily?" Maggy said, jumping out of the swing. "It's really fun. Barb's going to teach us all the cheers, so when we try out we'll know everything we're supposed to do."

I shook my head. "I'm not exactly the cheerleader type."

"What do you mean?"

I laughed. "Whoever heard of a cheerleader taller than the basketball team?"

"Oh, Emily."

"Come on, Mag. Barb won't hang around all day waiting for you, you know," Sandy said. She was still standing in the Rhodeses' yard, as if she thought our grass might poison her. For all the attention Sandy paid to me, Maggy might just as well have been talking to a snail.

"Well, I have to go," Maggy said. She ran across our yard and vanished around the corner of her house, close on Sandy's heels.

I sat on my swing for a while watching Maggy's empty seat sway back and forth. From up the street I could hear voices shouting, "Sis boom ba! Rah rah rah! Go, team, go!" Sandy's voice was louder than anybody else's, and I could imagine her jumping up and down, her blond hair flying in perfect swirls around her face while Ginny, sweaty and red-faced, frizzy-haired and miserable, panted along beside her.

Glad I wasn't there, I got up and walked around our house and down our street, away from the cheerleading practice. I passed Sara's house without even looking at it. When I got to the corner, I stopped under a tall oak and stared up into its branches.

Last summer Maggy and I had built a tree house in the tree. Nothing really fancy, but it had been a nice place to sit on a hot day and read comics. In the fall, Froggy, Jeff, Bruce, and Tommy had ripped it down and taken the boards to build a hut in the woods across the train tracks. All winter, Maggy and I had talked about building a new one in the summer. We even got in trouble for passing notes about it in school. But by spring, Maggy had lost interest in things like tree houses, so all that was left was a couple of board steps nailed to the trunk. Feeling sentimental, I climbed up into the tree and sat down.

The train tracks shimmered below me in the heat and all around me an invisible chorus of grasshoppers thrummed away, making a drowsy rising and falling sort of noise. Leaning back against the trunk, I watched the clouds float by dragging pieces of themselves in wisps behind them.

A screen door slammed up the street and soon I saw Sara walking toward me, her head down, her hands in her back pockets. Completely unaware that I was sitting in the tree, she walked right underneath me, so close I could see the crooked white line her part made across the top of her head.

She stopped on the bank of the train tracks near the

bunker, her back to me, and stood there staring off into space. At that moment she seemed like a stranger. I had no idea what she was thinking about, whether she was mad or sad or glad.

To stir her up, I pursed my lips and gave a long, low wolf whistle. She jumped and turned around, her face angry, then puzzled when she saw no one. Trying not to laugh I whistled again.

"Who's that?" Sara shouted. "Where are you? You can't scare me, you creep!"

FIFTEEN

Looking in every direction but up, Sara came across the street, her fists clenched. "Who's whistling?" she yelled.

I tried to whistle again, but in the middle of it, I burst out laughing. Since Sara was now directly under me, she finally looked up.

"What are you trying to prove?" she shouted at me.

"Can't you take a joke?"

"Of course I can. If it's funny, that is."

I scowled down at her, expecting her to leave. I was sorry I'd seen her and even sorrier I'd decided to make up with her. Who needed a friend like her?

But she didn't walk away. Instead she stood at the bottom of the tree twisting one of the boards nailed to the trunk. "What's this for?" she asked.

"It was a step. Maggy and I used to have a tree house here."

"Oh." She twisted the board some more. "What happened to it?"

"Froggy and some other guys tore it down."

"I hate Froggy."

"Me too."

We looked at each other. I brushed an ant off my leg, and Sara scratched a mosquito bite on her arm. In the field across the train tracks the grasshoppers shrilled away and a truck bumped over the Calvert Road crossing.

"Want to come up?" I finally asked. "I'll show you where the platform used to be."

"Okay." Sara grabbed the step she'd been twisting and it came off in her hand. "No wonder Froggy tore it down. Pretty flimsy construction."

She jumped for a limb and hoisted herself up into the tree. I showed her where our boards had been nailed. "We even had a pulley so we could bring our lunches up. Once we put Maggy's cat in the basket and pulled him up, but he didn't like it. Maggy still has a scar on her arm from one of the scratches."

"Too bad it got torn down," Sara said.

"Yeah, but that's what happens."

We sat there for a while, not saying anything.

"Well," Sara said finally, "school starts the day after tomorrow."

"Don't remind me."

Sara returned her attention to her mosquito bite.

She'd scratched it till it bled, and now she was spitting on her finger and wiping the blood away. I can't stand seeing people pick at themselves like that, even though I sometimes do it myself.

"Emily?" Sara looked up at me.

"What?"

"How do you think I'd look without braids?"

"You aren't going to get your hair cut, are you?"

"Mom thinks I should wear it differently. She says my braids look ridiculous."

"Really? That's just what my mother said when I tried to braid mine."

"Well, what do you think, Em? Should I let her cut it or what?"

I looked at Sara closely, pleased that she wanted my opinion, and tried to imagine her with short hair. I had a feeling that she'd look as bad as I did last summer when my hair had been really short. People had called me "sonny" and "fella."

I shook my head. "Let her trim it, Sara, but leave it long. What if you walked into school on the first day and a teacher asked, 'Will the boy in the blue shirt take this to the office for me' and she was looking at you?"

Sara twisted one of her braids around her finger. "I don't really want to cut it at all. I've had braids all my life, you know? But at the same time, I don't want to look weird or anything. Isn't that dumb?"

I shook my head. I knew exactly how she felt. "Maybe you could just wear it hanging down like you did at Ginny's party. Lots of girls would give anything to have hair as long as yours."

"Really?"

I nodded. "You have beautiful hair."

"Oh, come on," Sara said, but she twisted her braid tighter around her finger and looked pleased.

"Just be glad you're not me. How would you feel if you had a bald spot and eight stitches in your head?"

Sara stared at my scalp. "Who stitched it up? Dr. Frankenstein?"

"Does it look that bad?"

She shrugged and looked down at her feet. "You were really brave to do that, you know. I mean, if it hadn't been for you, Em, they'd still be finding pieces of Jennifer down there."

We looked at the steel tracks shimmering in the sunlight. I shuddered, still not really up to thinking about how I'd felt running toward Jennifer, terrified I wouldn't get there in time.

"You'd have done the same thing," I said.

"Don't count on it. I was so scared I couldn't move."

"I didn't know you were scared of anything," I said. And, to tell the truth, I didn't *want* to know. I wanted Sara to be as tough inside as she was outside.

"I'm scared of a lot of things, if you want to know, Em," Sara went on. She turned her attention to another mosquito bite and scratched it vigorously. "You want to know when I was really terrified?"

I stared at her, not sure what to say. It was like Sara was turning herself inside out and letting all the rough edges show.

"At Ginny's party. When I first got there and nobody was dressed like I was and they all stared at me. And later when Mr. Barnett got mad at me. I was scared then, too. But you know what I was most scared of?"

I shook my head.

"That you were going to stay there. That I was going to have to leave all by myself and you wouldn't come, you'd just stay there and talk to Catherine Simpson or Maggy or somebody like that." She dug her nails into another bite. "If other kids liked me as much as mosquitoes do, I'd really be popular," she added.

"I didn't think you cared whether I came with you or not. I mean, you never even looked at me."

"I was afraid to look at you," Sara said. "I thought you might look away, you know, like you thought I was weird, too."

"Really? You really thought that?"

Sara nodded, her eyes still on her mosquito bites. "You're the best friend I've ever had, Em."

Suddenly I couldn't understand how I could ever have hated Sara as much as I had. She was my friend, my best friend, and I knew I could tell her anything about me, no matter how stupid it was, and she wouldn't laugh and she wouldn't blab it all over school. She'd understand. And she could trust me, too.

She looked at me then, and I smiled at her. Together maybe we'd make it through junior high school after all.

"Come on, Em, it's boring sitting here. Let's get a Coke at my house and play a game of checkers."

Taking a deep breath, I decided it was time for me to say something I'd been rehearsing for weeks. Looking Sara right in the eye, I said, "All summer long we've been playing checkers, Sara, and all summer long you've been winning. Well, let me tell you something. I'm sick of always losing and I'm sick of checkers! If you want to do something else, fine, I'll be happy to come over for a while. But no checkers!"

Sara looked surprised. "I thought you liked checkers," she said. "How was I supposed to know you hated playing? You never said anything, you know. I can't read your mind, Emily. I thought you looked at it as a challenge."

"Well, I don't. And I'm saying something now. I HATE CHECKERS!"

"Okay, okay, you don't have to get so excited about it. We can always find something else to do. How about chess? I could teach you how to play."

"No, not chess. If I can't think far enough ahead to play checkers, how could I ever learn chess? How about riding our bikes somewhere? Like down to the creek? We could pack our lunches and have a picnic."

Sara grinned. "Why not?"

We climbed down from the tree, and, as I started up the street behind her, I tried hard to remember how I had walked before I met Sara.

From out of the Shadows...
Stories Filled with Mystery
and Suspense by
MARY DOWNING HAHN

TIME FOR ANDREW
72469-3/$3.99 US/$4.99 Can

DAPHNE'S BOOK
72355-7/$3.99 US/$4.99 Can

THE TIME OF THE WITCH
71116-8/ $3.99 US/ $4.99 Can

STEPPING ON THE CRACKS
71900-2/ $3.99 US/ $4.99 Can

THE DEAD MAN IN INDIAN CREEK
71362-4/ $3.99 US/ $4.99 Can

THE DOLL IN THE GARDEN
70865-5/ $3.50 US/ $4.25 Can

FOLLOWING THE MYSTERY MAN
70677-6/ $3.99 US/ $4.99 Can

TALLAHASSEE HIGGINS
70500-1/ $3.99 US/ $4.99 Can

WAIT TILL HELEN COMES
70442-0/ $3.99 US/ $4.99 Can

THE SPANISH KIDNAPPING DISASTER
71712-3/ $3.99 US/ $4.99 Can

THE JELLYFISH SEASON
71635-6/ $3.50 US/ $4.25 Can

Coming Soon
THE SARA SUMMER
72354-9/ $3.99 US/ $4.99 Can

Buy these books at your local bookstore or use this coupon for ordering:

Mail to: Avon Books, Dept BP, Box 767, Rte 2, Dresden, TN 38225   C
Please send me the book(s) I have checked above.
❑ My check or money order— no cash or CODs please— for $_____is enclosed
(please add $1.50 to cover postage and handling for each book ordered— Canadian residents
add 7% GST).
❑ Charge my VISA/MC Acct#_____Exp Date_____
Minimum credit card order is two books or $6.00 (please add postage and handling charge of
$1.50 per book — Canadian residents add 7% GST). For faster service, call
1-800-762-0779. Residents of Tennessee, please call 1-800-633-1607. Prices and numbers
are subject to change without notice. Please allow six to eight weeks for delivery.

Name_____
Address_____
City_____State/Zip_____
Telephone No._____   MDH 0395

Read All the Stories by
Beverly Cleary

☐ **HENRY HUGGINS**
70912-0 ($3.99 US/ $4.99 Can)

☐ **HENRY AND BEEZUS**
70914-7 ($3.99 US/ $4.99 Can)

☐ **HENRY AND THE CLUBHOUSE**
70915-5 ($3.99 US/ $4.99 Can)

☐ **ELLEN TEBBITS**
70913-9 ($3.99 US/ $4.99 Can)

☐ **HENRY AND RIBSY**
70917-1 ($3.99 US/ $4.99 Can)

☐ **BEEZUS AND RAMONA**
70918-X ($3.99 US/ $4.99 Can)

☐ **RAMONA AND HER FATHER**
70916-3 ($3.99 US/ $4.99 Can)

☐ **MITCH AND AMY**
70925-2 ($3.99 US/ $4.99 Can)

☐ **RUNAWAY RALPH**
70953-8 ($3.99 US/ $4.99 Can)

☐ **RAMONA QUIMBY, AGE 8**
70956-2 ($3.99 US/ $4.99 Can)

☐ **RIBSY**
70955-4 ($3.99 US/ $4.99 Can)

☐ **STRIDER**
71236-9 ($3.99 US/ $4.99 Can)

☐ **HENRY AND THE PAPER ROUTE**
70921-X ($3.99 US/ $4.99 Can)

☐ **RAMONA AND HER MOTHER**
70952-X ($3.99 US/ $4.99 Can)

☐ **OTIS SPOFFORD**
70919-8 ($3.99 US/ $4.99 Can)

☐ **THE MOUSE AND THE MOTORCYCLE**
70924-4 ($3.99 US/ $4.99 Can)

☐ **SOCKS**
70926-0 ($3.99 US/ $4.99 Can)

☐ **EMILY'S RUNAWAY IMAGINATION**
70923-6 ($3.99 US/ $4.99 Can)

☐ **MUGGIE MAGGIE**
71087-0 ($3.99 US/ $4.99 Can)

☐ **RAMONA THE PEST**
70954-6 ($3.99 US/ $4.99 Can)

☐ **RALPH S. MOUSE**
70957-0 ($3.99 US/ $4.99 Can)

☐ **DEAR MR. HENSHAW**
70958-9 ($3.99 US/ $4.99 Can)

☐ **RAMONA THE BRAVE**
70959-7 ($3.99 US/ $4.99 Can)

Buy these books at your local bookstore or use this coupon for ordering:

Mail to: Avon Books, Dept BP, Box 767, Rte 2, Dresden, TN 38225   C
Please send me the book(s) I have checked above.
❑ My check or money order— no cash or CODs please— for $_____is enclosed
(please add $1.50 to cover postage and handling for each book ordered— Canadian residents
add 7% GST).
❑ Charge my VISA/MC Acct#_____Exp Date_____
Minimum credit card order is two books or $6.00 (please add postage and handling charge of
$1.50 per book — Canadian residents add 7% GST). For faster service, call
1-800-762-0779. Residents of Tennessee, please call 1-800-633-1607. Prices and numbers
are subject to change without notice. Please allow six to eight weeks for delivery.

Name_____
Address_____
City_____State/Zip_____
Telephone No._____   BEV 0195